# THE SPACEPORT GAMBIT

## SCOUNDREL SPACE BOOK ONE

# M. SCOTT DAVIDS

READ MORE ADVENTURES AT
# WWW.SCOUNDRELSPACE.COM

Published by Astra Vici Press

Cover design by jcelebdesign.com
Book design by Matt Davids
Edited by Jonathan Oliver

Paperback ISBN: 978-1-952089-13-8
Hardcover ISBN: 978-1-952089-14-5
Printed in the United States of America

For my six-year-old self.
Sorry, it took so long.

# PART 1:
# THE DEAL

Deal, deal, run the risk
Place your bets or take a chance
You only live once
                            - The Poet Loam

# 1

JORDANA SALAMANCA eased up on the stick and let her fighter roll. She focused, closing out the chaos of beeps and shouts in her earpiece. The fighter's HUD displayed the pirate fighter. One more slight adjustment. The HUD lit up with a red target indicator. The word 'LOCK' flashed at Jordana. She squeezed the trigger.

Bright bolts of crackling energy spilled out of her fighter craft. The bolts touched the pirate fighter. It burst into flame, scattering debris through space.

"Thank you, Ghost Leader," came a staticky voice. "I thought he had me."

"Roger, that. Stay sharp." Jordana peeled off. She only took a moment to check the wellbeing of her squadron. They were doing well, but that had been a close call. She quickly got a read on her wingman. Excellent. He still had her back.

Jordana sought another target. She switched between sensor and visual scanning. There. Nine hundred thirty-four meters away a pirate fighter arced wide. Why? She looked. He was trying to get a bead on Ghost Three. Not going to happen.

"Eyes on," she said and she locked a sensor beam on the enemy craft.

"Roger, that. Got your sensor mark," came the reply from her wingman.

Jordana swung her fighter to intercept. The HUD searched for the target and placed a yellow outline around the pirate fighter. She flipped a couple of switches and throttled hard. This one was not getting away.

"Evasive action!" her wingman's voice screamed in her ear just as an alarm sounded. Jordana's instincts kicked in and she slammed the control stick to one side. Her ship spun and dove as bright energy bolts streaked past.

"Got a lock!" Her wingman again. She could now see the pirate craft. He was on her tight. Her display showed her wingman as well. He was closing.

An explosion. The pirate craft was ripped into tiny bits. "Nice shooting, Ghost Two!" Jordana yelled. "Where did he come from?"

"An old navigational beacon. Used the magnetic field to hide."

No time to think. Jordana checked her scopes. The pirate she was after before was still hunting Ghost Three. "Follow me in." She would not lose a pilot today.

"Roger, that."

She reoriented her craft and re-established the sensor beam. The HUD lit up. The pirate peeled off from Ghost Three in a wild vertical spinning climb. *This one's good*, she thought as she struggled to get a target lock.

She followed the craft into the climb and punched her augmenting thrusters. "You're not getting away today, my friend." Cold death entered Jordana's eyes. Target lock. She had him.

She scored a direct hit on the craft's fuel tanks. Fiery pieces of the pirate craft scattered over a wide area. "Ghost Three, you should be clear."

"Thanks, boss," a crackly female voice said in Jordana's ear.

Jordana maneuvered her craft to survey the conflict zone. She sent out a wide scanning beam. The HUD outlined asteroids, old beacons, fighter craft debris, her squadron, and enemy craft in various colors. The *Apollo*, massive and gleaming in the light of a distant star, hung off the fighter engagement zone and defended herself when necessary. Captain Pratt waited. Waited for Ghost Squadron to locate the pirate base. Fighters had to dock, it must be close.

Jordana was happy to see her squadron had the upper hand. Ghost Seven had just obliterated a pirate fighter. But where was the pirate's base? A ship or an outpost had to be tucked in among these asteroids and old beacons.

"Ghost Two, begin an intensive scanning beam 23-45-78 mark 4. I'll scan 24-56-43 mark 8."

"Got it, Ghost Leader."

Her scopes displayed reams of information. Nothing. "Switching mark 6." She wanted these pirates to pay.

"Switching mark 2." She heard in her ear. Ghost Two picked up on her scanning pattern. Great work.

Nothing, nothing. Still nothing. "Switching mark 10." It had to be here she thought.

"Switching mark 12." Ghost Two crackled. "Wait..."

"What is it?" She nearly jumped.

"Asteroid with an odd gravitational reading. Sending data."

Jordana took in the info from Ghost Two. She saw it. The gravitational patterns were all wrong for an asteroid that size. "Nice job! Let's swing around."

"Aye, aye!"

Jordana's fighter swam through space. The asteroid rushed up to meet her, huge and pock marked with streaks of glittering indigos and otherworldly turquoise. Sensors showed it was high in osmium and iridium. The perfect hiding spot. With a flick of her wrist, her craft skirted the giant rock. Ghost Two stayed close with her.

There she was. A Colossus Class Destroyer retrofitted with fighter bays and a Lapakana Tractor Beam Array. The quintessential pirate ship.

"They've spotted us." Ghost Two's voice dripped with excitement.

"Roger that. I'm sending data to the *Apollo*, now! Follow me." Jordana punched a few buttons and then jabbed the stick down.

The fighter crafts dove in a spiral. They flattened out and passed under the belly of the pirate vessel.

Jordana squeezed off a couple of shots as did Ghost Two. The beams bounced off invisible shielding. They couldn't hurt it yet, but soon. After the bursts, Jordana executed a hard turn underneath the asteroid. Just in time. The pirate ship blasted a chunk out of the asteroid right behind the two tiny fighters.

As Jordana's craft emerged on the opposite side of the massive asteroid, she saw it. The *Apollo* majestically maneuvered into attack position. Captain Pratt wasted no time once he received the data they sent.

Jordana pulled her fighter into a steep climb with Ghost Two right behind. She positioned her fighter high above the *Apollo* and watched the ship crest the asteroid. "Set your scanning, Ghost Two. Watch our backs."

"Roger, that."

The *Apollo* rained down a hell of sizzling energy bolts upon the pirate vessel. The pirate ship returned fire and began to maneuver away, but it was no match for the Apollo.

Jordana switched her scanner beam to the pirate vessel. "Shields are down." The *Apollo* did quick work. "Standby, Ghost Two. We'll clean up any escape pods or craft."

"Aye, aye."

"Ghost Three, how goes the fight?" Jordana checked in.

"Only two left and they are on the run. Should have them soon."

"Excellent. Once you finish them off, regroup on my position."

"Roger, boss."

Jordana watched as the pirate ship broke apart with a huge explosion. Debris sprayed out in a kilometers-wide arc. One gigantic piece of the ship fractured, spitting a kaleidoscope of colors into the dark of space. Another piece collided with the asteroid and fragmented into thousands of shards.

"Reading escape pods, Ghost Leader," Ghost Two informed her. Indicators appeared on her screen.

"Let's clean up this mess." Jordana throttled hard toward the fray.

# 2

THE DISTANT MOUNTAINS were quiet and birds chirped above the corporate types on lunch breaks. The open-air plaza felt like a room in one of the climate-controlled skyscrapers that surrounded it.

Yet Gwen was stormy. The presentation had not gone well. The automatic glass door fled from her presence and she entered the sunlight. Her vision formed a tunnel and her mind jumbled a flurry of half-formed thoughts.

All the logical arguments backed up with data had been ridiculed and rejected. Why? Because it didn't "feel" or "seem" or some other mealymouthed word from that Nigellus Gardner. The board members were listening until he started babbling and contradicting and interjecting.

Gwen knew he hated her and wanted her to fail, but this was ridiculous. Couldn't the others see? Her data were correct. The fringe sectors were growing and corporate investment now would mean huge profits later. Why couldn't they see?

Nigellus Gardner was why. The board and Srinivas were favoring him now for some reason. Sure, Gardner was smart and smooth. He made PanGalacta a lot of money, but so did she.

With Srinivas most likely retiring in a year, many of the VPs were showing off. It made sense Gardner was laying it on thick. What did he say? "If it's such a good idea, why don't you buy it?" He just wanted Gwen out of the picture. Why that pompous...

Sunlight played in the leaves of a row of maple saplings. The sight pierced her tunnel vision. The swirl of hateful thoughts slowed. The rush of anger and frustration crested. Gwen wondered if she was performing for the position, too. No, her presentation made sense. Well, maybe she was performing a little bit. Being CEO of PanGalacta would be a career capstone. It was bold, maybe bolder than normal with the CEO position riding on who could come up with the next big thing.

However, her proposal to revitalize the abandoned spaceport on Erebus was sound and backed up with data trends showing that the sector needed a spaceport. PanGalacta owned the port already thanks to the AI War settlement. A sizable investment would be needed since it had sat unused for seventy-five years, but it was worth it.

Gwen looked up. The air was clean and fresh. Butterflies floated in lazy loops. What a beautiful day. To think so many people were angry, upset, and striving in the glass towers around her. Why was she so angry? She had been an exec for a long time and project ideas got shot down all the time for all kinds of reasons.

Something was different. She believed in the project. That spaceport would help thousands of traders and would perform vital services to commerce in the sector. Why had that asset been left to rust? Simply because it was far away and needed more than a hundred billion in investments? That hadn't stopped the company's investment in the Mongo Lai station, though that was closer to earth.

It was probably because Gardner didn't think of it and he couldn't give her a big win in the current climate. She was stuck. If the board favored Gardner, the project was dead. *Why don't you buy it?* Isn't that what he said? *Why don't you buy it?*

Gwen shook her head and looked at the mountains. Tiny silver flecks moved far away in the sky. That's impossible. How much would a spaceport cost? As she thought it, the word 'impossible' riled her. In her career, she had tackled problems many thought impossible. But buying a spaceport? If something was impossible, that would be it.

She sat on the low quallcrete wall. She thought slowly now, if not rationally. She'd have to put together a buying group. Whoa, was she thinking about buying the spaceport?

Well, why not? She had the business experience to build a pool of investors. She currently managed 517,841 employees on forty-eight planets in her division of PanGalacta. She had overseen construction projects on Resheph One and Dangun as well as in Ulaanbaatar.

It was a gamble, but it made sense. Her numbers were right. The sector was ripe for a spaceport. What about her career? If Nigellus Gardner became CEO, her position may mysteriously not be needed any longer. Would he do that? Hmm, in a heartbeat. He had always been threatened by her.

*If it's such a good idea, why don't you buy it?* Well, Mr. Gardner, why not? Gwen got up and with purpose walked back to the PanGalacta headquarters.

# 3

"HOW MUCH DOES a spaceport cost?"

Gwen tilted her head. "Would you be shocked if I said a lot?"

"No, not one bit." Liam put down his fork and wiped his mouth with a napkin. His elbow brushed the back of her hand slightly as he had raised his arms. The kitchen table forced them to be close together. She liked it. The large dining room table didn't feel right without their girls.

She watched his eyes. She had just dropped a bomb on him; a bomb blowing apart their comfortable lives, blowing apart his business. She was asking a lot. Was she still seriously considering this?

"Knowing you, you've been thorough. I'm guessing you have some details."

"Yes." Gwen indeed had been thorough. "I discussed it with the board. The sale price would be fifty billion. PanGalacta would finance a loan with a two percent down payment. I'm in talks with Raiffeisen-Haberfeld for another fifty billion loan as long as I provide the spaceport as collateral. I'm estimating at least that in repairs. I need other investors and fast, but I can get them."

Liam blinked. "PanGalacta will finance with a two percent down payment?" She could see his gears turning.

"Contingent on me resigning from PanGalacta and a thirty percent equity stake. It was Gardner's idea."

"I see." Liam leaned back. She watched his eyes consider the ceiling then the wall behind her. "He's just getting rid of you."

"I know."

"You're giving up the chance to become CEO."

"I know."

"It'll be a big change for all of us."

"I know."

Liam chewed more than his dinner. He nodded slowly. Gwen took a deep breath. "All you have to do is say no and I won't do it."

"We've been married long enough for me to know that."

She smiled. She loved the way he tilted his head and grinned.

"We are in a pretty good place with Chloe now at university. I could talk with Greg and Saheed. We have a lot of projects coming up, but it doesn't really matter where I live." Liam reached for a dinner roll.

Oh, how she loved this man. How many times had her career pulled them from one place to another? He always accommodated and reordered his career. "As I said, just say the word and I drop it."

"Do you really want this?" He fixed his eyes on her.

She looked him in the eyes. Those blue eyes... "Yes, I do."

Liam took a bite of the roll. "Then let's do it."

She grabbed his hand.

"You'll need more than investors, you'll need a team."

"I know people." She smiled.

# Ч

THE HEADS-UP-DISPLAY filled her vision with sick reports, progress reports, timetables, live video from multiple branch offices, inquiries, calendars, requests, news, and more.

The freighter *Ocelus* had missed a scheduled check in. With a slight movement of a finger, she alerted GU Patrols in the area. A nine point three earthquake on Callahan Zou near the capital. Waving fingers initiated welfare checks on all employees and assigned medical and construction personnel to evaluate the site.

The data flowed and Bao Li sifted through it. Acting and reacting, faster and faster.

Some data were irrelevant. She tossed those to the side with a flick of her wrist. The important bits were saved and assigned to appropriate managers or authorities. Her decisions were made in the blink of an eye. Irrelevant. Irrelevant. Assigned. Assigned. Assigned. Irrelevant. Only every few minutes did she let one report or image hover in her vision for more than a few seconds.

The multiple feeds shrank, moved to the sides and an image of an orca in a water tank grew larger. Ports along the killer whale's spine connected it to a mass of cables and wires. The giant floating creature surrounded by vivid blue water and yards of cables drew a picture Bao found beautiful yet unsettlingly so.

"Titus, are you well today? One of the engineers noted you are not acting like yourself." Bao's voice contained genuine concern.

"Just a little tired, I think. Trouble concentrating is all." The computer-generated voice conveyed the character of its owner as well as a touch of melancholy, Bao thought.

"Your medical staff have been notified and will be with you shortly." Even as she said it she knew the cetacean lab technicians were running a full workup on him. "I'm shutting down your workday and reassigning your tasks."

"No need, please. I can still be useful."

"It's okay, Titus. It happens to us all. No need to worry."

The whale seemed to think for a moment. "Yes, ma'am. Maybe some rest is what I need."

"That's right. You get some rest. I'll check in tomorrow."

"Thank you, Bao."

The image of the orca faded into a small rectangle and the other feeds came back. She quickly reassigned Titus' duties to a humpback named Sadie and a dolphin named Horatio.

Bao's eyes dashed, catching up on what she missed. An explosion on Sallis 9. Reconfiguring delivery schedules. Several employees had fallen ill with a fever and rash on Aglaurus. Notifying the Office of Epidemiology. A freighter had arrived two hours late to the port on Uberaba. Adjusting timetables.

A countdown started in the corner of her display. She hurried through a few more tasks. Irrelevant. Assigned. Assigned. Assigned. Then the display went dark. She blinked. Her mandatory fifteen-minute break. She stood up out of the padded chair.

She paced in a circle around the chair. The stark white room was featureless, save for the outline of a door with lock release. Her legs and back liked the movement. She wasn't hungry yet, this was the first break of the day. She did drink some water. Once she had let herself become dehydrated. She wasn't going through that again. Time was almost up.

Bao sat back in the chair and arranged her hair in a comfortable position. Her panel beeped. A personal call. Interesting. She checked the ID. Gwendolyn Shepherd Davis.

What? Her boss' boss' boss' boss calling her? She'd done something wrong. She was ashamed. She must speed up her work.

"Bao Li, Operations." Bao's voice wasn't strong.

"Ms. Li, it is a pleasure to finally speak to you. Your work is outstanding and you come highly recommended."

"Thank you. You honor me." Bao slightly bowed her head.

"I have a proposal for you." Gwen's smile was warm and friendly.

# 5

BRAEDEN FOSTER stared blankly. Two entire walls of his office were windows. He found it hard not to stare out of them at least a few times a day. He stood only a few centimeters away from the triglass. The city seethed beneath him.

Countless aircars, transports, dogesleds, skiffs, and pods swarmed in chaotic patterns like mosquitos around physics-defying buildings. Heat vapors rose in tremendous sheets distorting the cityscape like a madman's painting. The yellowish-green glow of the day gave way to the reddish-green glow of the evening.

How god awful. To think when he was first escorted up and shown his new office, he loved it. Well, he loved the promotion, the money, and the prestige. But this?

A large freighter pierced the cloud layer in the distance and thousands of gnat-like drones glided up to meet it. Braeden could just make out the freighter's name – *Chung-hoon* the symbols on the hull read. The massive metal beast completed the dreary skyline.

"File compiling done." A metallic voice slit the silence and halted his thoughts.

"Send copies to Jenkins, Soo, Hamersfeld, Filoni, and Goggins with the note: 'Final numbers needed, yet third-quarter profits are strong.'"

"Executing. Done." The computer's voice stated.

Was that all he needed to do today? More than enough. Ten hours had passed since he came in this morning. He was ready to go home.

Before he turned away from the window, a soft chirp sounded in his ear and an indicator appeared in the vision of his left eye. His personal comm channel. He flipped a mental switch.

"Hello."

"Braeden, how have you been?" asked Gwendolyn Shepherd Davis.

"Doing well. How about yourself? It's been a few years."

"I'm well. It has been four years if my math is right."

"How can I help you?" Braeden was curious.

"I need a financial wizard for a new ventu—"

"I'm in."

"It's risky and you don't know the details yet."

"Doesn't matter. I'm in. Send any details you have to me now. I'll look them over, but I'm in."

"Great. Sending them now."

Green, blue, and red indicators appeared in Braeden's vision. Files downloading.

# 6

IN THE LITTLE CAPSULE hanging somewhere between the Janus/Epimetheus ring, his hands shook. The thirty-eight minutes and forty-two seconds of terror were over. The indicator light on the panel switched to green and he knew he had done it. The Cassini Station with all 59,000 people on board wouldn't lose stabilization, break apart, and plunge into Saturn. Now, he had ninety-eight hours of free time until he had to face the terror again.

But this was nothing new to David Mercer. He had run the procedure hundreds of times. He knew it backward and forward, but the terror remained each time. Of course, AI should do a job like this. He could write one to do it, he knew he could. Though, since the AI War, no one trusted them and that meant a person had to be out here. Well, if they didn't replace the person with a dolphin.

David hated the thought of losing this job to a dolphin, no matter how intelligent the creature was. Increasing the intelligence of cetaceans was an exciting field and the scientists were making incredible strides. Soon uplifted animal interfaces would be piloting most large interstellar crafts, so it was said. Each time his six-month tour on the Proximo was over, he heard the rumors. He tried not to listen. He liked this job.

Six months on but six months off and a cool million in the bank each time a tour ended. Besides, he was the expert. He had helped upgrade the old system and streamline the new one. This was his eleventh tour. No one else had completed more than two, and one person committed suicide.

.

Must have been a scary few days on Cassini Station. Getting someone on the capsule was tricky.

After the procedure was completed he always thought about the AI and the dolphin. Where others hated the isolation, David thrived on it. He always had so much to do.

He had the sum of all human knowledge at his fingertips. A touch of a few buttons brought any book, movie, or music he wished right to him. He could research any topic from literature to microbiology to quantum information theory and more.

Then there was the view. Saturn and the rings swirling in the heavens and the star-specked infinity. If Melville's young Platonist lost his identity gazing upon the ocean, what would this view have done to him?

David always had research projects. Computer science was his life. After his first two tours, he produced a book called, *Problematic Data Structures: A House of Digital Cards*. It had won him some praise and a couple of speaking engagements and a guest lecture at the National University of Singapore's Vargas-Sai School of Advanced Computer Science.

The profits from the book were modest, but the name recognition is what he craved. At first, that is. The luster soon wore off and he preferred not to attend conferences and lectures. He spent most of his six months off at his condo in Ares City on Mars or the townhouse in Sydney back on Earth.

However, his writing had dwindled and his research projects had faltered and nearly stopped. What would he do with his ninety-eight hours this week? Finish reading *The Brothers Karamazov*? (He'd started it two - or was it three? – years ago.) Work on his latest book, *The Twelve New Dimensions of Cryptography*?

As he calmed down and showered, thoughts of these things didn't fill his mind. He had found new pastimes recently. During the last few tours, he had spent the majority of the downtime watching videos of people falling, videos about toys he played with as a child, video games, and porn, lots of porn.

He settled down with a Thai rice dish and brought up the videos of his favorite porn star. But there were no new videos. Running late he guessed. He clicked over and found a video compilation of people dropping things at their day jobs. After that, a video about a cartoon he watched when he was seven or eight years old, *The Adventures of Captain Cosmo*. "From beyond time and from the farthest reaches of space..." the intro began. The videos weren't all that good, but they calmed his nerves, so he could fall asleep.

There were still no videos from his favorite channel. *Weird. Must be an issue. She'll post soon no doubt.* He filled his downtime with other porn and videos. He tried listening to music once, but gave up and went back to the viewer for more videos.

Then before he knew it, the time had come. He calmed himself and got into position behind the mad scientist computer panel. The thirty-eight minutes and forty-two seconds of terror began again. His concentration was intense and the indicator light switched green. It was over. His stomach growled. Time to relax.

He couldn't believe it. What was he going to do? Still no new videos. There were always new videos each week, now it had been two without. His heart shuttered slightly and he felt sick. Sick because there were no new videos from one particular woman? Sick because that thought made him sick?

He threw himself into other porn. Hours and hours of it. Something was wrong. He needed something else. He tried reading *The Brothers Karamazov* but couldn't concentrate. He stared at a blinking cursor at the end of a sentence that read, 'Cryptography truly entered a new era during...' but he couldn't finish it. He thought about calling his brother. They hadn't spoken in a few weeks or was it a few months, a year? What would Mom think? What would Mom think about the porn? Oh, god...

The little capsule shrank and became more claustrophobic. He hyperventilated. A panic attack? Oh, no. The medical sensors would pick this up soon and Command would check to see if he was okay. He couldn't have that. They'd surely replace him with a dolphin. He started meditating, slowing his breathing, clearing his mind.

Beep, beep.

"You okay, Dave?" came the voice. It was Command Officer Yanna Kuznetsov.

"Yeah, I'm okay."

"Anything we need to know about?"

"No, I'm fine. Got a little worked up, but I'm good."

"Are you sure? Your heart and breathing looked a bit off."

"I'm good."

"Logs show you have been pretty isolated. You know the guidelines suggest you stay in contact with friends and family while you're on a tour."

"I know. I'm okay really."

"Sure thing. If you need some company, we could play chess sometime."

"Thanks, but really, I'm okay. Maybe another day. I'm good, really."

"Okay, if you say so. We'll check in again in one hour to make sure."

"Got it. Sounds good."

"Okay, take it easy, Dave. Command out."

Whoa, that was close. He just needed to calm down and not to think. But think he did. All the time he showered and all night in bed. Why was he so upset? It was just some videos, right? Not a big deal. So what was it?

Yanna was probably right. He was too isolated. There were guidelines after all and they had been put in place for a reason. It was good hearing her voice, even if it was an official check-in. But something else bothered him. He didn't want to admit it at first, but then he did. He didn't like the way he was spending his downtime. All drive had disappeared. He was comfortable and making good money. He didn't have to try hard anymore. Soon after he fell asleep.

As the capsule's lights brightened, David got up and went about his routine. The thoughts were still there. He needed to do something else. He needed a change. He shaved. Wow, he had stopped that too? How could he have let himself get into a place like this? Wasting so much time? Not caring about himself? He needed a change.

Ding. A new message? Who could it be? He sat at the computer screen and opened his personal messages. A new one from Gwendolyn Shepherd Davis. Gwen? They had worked together ten years ago, no fifteen. He liked her. She was smart and asked the right questions of programmers and engineers. A good exec. Why was she messaging? He clicked play.

"Dave, hopefully, you remember me. We worked on the Jade-Thompson project about fourteen years ago. Something's come up and I need a great computer guy. You were the first person I thought of. If you're up for a challenge, message me. Cheers, Gwen."

The first person she thought of? A challenge? He did need a change, right? He took a deep breath. It wouldn't hurt to see what the job was, would it? He didn't have to say, yes. He could just learn more. But after all, a dolphin could do this job.

He started a reply.

# 7

GWEN WALKED BRISKLY down a covered quallcrete ramp and emerged into bright sunlight. The small rectangular park nestled between giant spires of triglass and burasteel.

"Thank you for taking a quick call," she said into the device in her hand. Gwen's device displayed a split screen of Bao and Braeden. They both nodded.

"I'm grateful to have you both onboard. Raiffeisen-Haberfeld came through with the loan. We have forty-nine billion to work with right now, but it won't go very far I'm afraid."

"It's a start." Braeden's voice crackled a bit. "I'm working my contacts for investors and we'll have to start thinking about legal seriously."

"I know. Keep on it." Gwen acknowledged. "Bao, as chief procurement officer, what's your status?"

"Mercer and Braeden sent me lists of what they need to get started. I've begun locating equipment and items. I just need the funds."

Gwen stopped near a park bench and looked down at the two little faces on the device. "Well, now you have them. Braeden, make sure she has what she needs. The money should be in the account now."

"Roger that, boss." Braeden's eyes flicked as if he was looking at something inside his head.

"Okay, I just wanted to let you know I got the loan. There are a few more people I'd like to on-board if they are available. Keep up the great work."

Bao and Braeden nodded and the screen went black. Gwen took a deep breath and looked up to the sky. Dealing with Raiffeisen-Haberfeld had taken a lot out of her, but she was ready for more.

# 8

THE YELLOW LEAVES cascaded around him like rain. A dusty and scratchy rain, but like rain nonetheless as the crumbled shells fell with the frequency and intensity of a downpour. Ridley Lopez shielded his eyes and emerged from the shower still on the path.

The leaves distracted Ridley and he wondered what type of tree had so many leaves. Then he caught himself. He came here to think, but not about trees.

Autumn already. Where had the time gone? His family relocated here nearly two years ago now. What did he have to show for it? The call from Gwen Davis and the job offer dominated the last few days.

He enjoyed the botanical gardens and he could think here. Besides, his wife told him to get out of the apartment. Of course, she was right. He needed to think and to think quickly. The offer wouldn't stay on the table forever.

It all seemed so complicated. What were the complications? Brecklyn thought he should take the job. He hated his job now. The kids would be disrupted, but that could be dealt with. What was holding him back?

The trail dead-ended at a Japanese rock garden. The wave-like lines held his eyes. He was afraid. He knew that and could admit it, but afraid of what?

Moving? No, they'd moved four times since they got married. Upsetting the kids? No, they could continue school over comms. Distance learning was extremely common. Leaving this job? No, he hated it and it was clear he wasn't going to be promoted anytime soon. Brecklyn? No, she had already told him to take the job. What then?

Ridley wandered back up the path past the mystery tree with yellow leaves. This time he skirted the cone of dusty rain trying not to crush the wildflowers just off the trail. Then he started down another path toward the koi pond. What then?

Reeds, the color of new baseball mitt leather, lined two sides of the pond. The far side nearly touched the great triglass dome surrounding the gardens. Real rain scourged the outside of the dome with a fury only reserved for those in Tartarus.

What then? The fish – enormous "koi-not-koi" as his kids called them – stirred the water.

Was it Gwen? No, he enjoyed working with her. Of course, they'd only worked together for less than a year. She said she was impressed by him. High praise from someone like Gwen Shepherd Davis to be sure.

That the spaceport may fail? No. Well, at least, not really. It'd be a bump in the road, but he could recover his career. What then? A giant red koi-not-koi puckered across the pond. His presence was drawing a crowd, but he didn't have any food for them.

Chief Operations Officer? No... Wait, maybe that was it. What if he failed? Failing at such a high level would mean his career would be over. Who'd hire a failed COO to be a director?

That was it, wasn't it? He was afraid to fail. He'd spent his entire professional career preparing for the top jobs at a spaceport and now he was afraid. Well, that wouldn't do, now would it?

# 9

"Mushrooms."

"I'm sorry?"

"Mushrooms. You asked about my family's business. I grew up on Hopkins, so my family's business was... um... is in mushrooms."

"Oh, you grew up there? There was a terrible accident, wasn't there?"

The chestnut curls of the woman on the monitor bobbed as she spoke. The green of her eyes was like the Vilbus butterflies on New Watersdown or at least that's what Edison thought.

He was nervous. "Yes, yes there was. The colony transport ship *Evander* exploded in low orbit. Thankfully all the colonists had been offloaded. Otherwise, my family and I would have been killed. Of course, the ship's crew was killed, which was horrible."

"And radiation flooded the atmosphere?"

"Yeah, that's right. We all fled into the large caverns and they shielded us. I mean, I don't remember much. I was only four at the time."

"I remember we learned about it in school. I would have been two when it happened. The mushrooms were in the caverns?" The curls bobbed up and down and her mouth moved just right.

"Yes, my parents and some of the others were the first to discover them. It was a good thing too because we had to live on them until we got other food sources."

"That's amazing. What an incredible childhood. Mine was so boring." She rolled her eyes and carried out the 'or' sound. "But you became an engineer, not a mycologist or a phytopathologist?"

"Yeah, I loved tinkering with the colony's air filters and the fertilizing systems. I designed several systems before I went to univer—"

"I've always loved science. But your parents studied fungi, right?"

"Well, yes. I mean, my father was a zoologist, but quickly became an expert on Hopkins mushrooms out of necessity. My mother helped launch the export business. She is so good at organizing and dealing with people. Actually, she was just elected planetary governor."

"Oh my god! Are you serious? Your mom's a planetary governor? Amazing!" The green of her eyes sparkled and played in the sea of white.

Edison was even more nervous now. He should be asking her more about herself, but she seemed to like his answers. Maybe something would come of this? "Yes, she's incredible. I've always been inspired by her drive and her work ethi—"

"What party is she?" The curls bobbed.

"Free Liberty."

The curls stopped bobbing. The words 'Chat Ended' appeared then dissolved into hundreds of tiny pictures of different women with 'Available to Chat' underneath.

Edison slammed his fist on the console. His heart screamed. Politics are so touchy. Why did he mention his mother? Wait. Wait! No need to info dump on a first chat.

He looked at the screen. He could choose another and start chatting. He quickly looked over the images on the screen. They all fit his profile settings. Age range twenty-two to thirty-two, light brown to dark brown hair, and green eyes. No, he had already chatted with three women tonight. He should relax. He had to work in the morning.

His dinner was a joyless affair. He flipped TainNet channels and ran several searches. Seventy-four thousand channels and there was nothing good on. Probably his sour mood.

As he was about to go to bed, he heard a chime. Who's calling? he wondered. He moved to the screen by his bed. Gwendolyn Shepherd Davis? Had something gone wrong with the Ulaanbaatar build? No, he did his best work on that job. He flipped the channel open.

"Hope I'm not bothering you, Edison. I didn't expect you to answer."

"Just caught me. How can I help you? Is the Ulaanbaatar Complex still suiting the company's needs?"

"Of course, it is. You designed and built one of the most impressive projects I've ever seen."

Edison nearly blushed.

Gwen took a breath. "I was so impressed with your work, I'd like to offer you a job. It's the most challenging project I've ever tackled and I need the best engineer I know."

Edison raised an eyebrow. "What's the job?"

# 10

No telling how many of the rare darwood trees perished when Srinivas' office was decorated. Every square inch, save the giant windows, was covered in the luscious brown wood. No expense had been spared for the CEO of PanGalacta.

Gwen stood tall and erect over the large desk as Srinivas quickly scanned the information displayed on a datapad. The little man looked up at her.

"Are you sure about this?"

"More than you know." Gwen decided her course of action and set her will. Was it easy resigning from the company she'd worked for for more than twenty-five years? Was it easy signing over a billion unions? No, but just because a thing is difficult doesn't mean you shouldn't do it.

The old man frowned. "Very well. I accept your resignation." He stood up and walked around the desk to face Gwen. "Buying that old spaceport."

"Yes, Srinivas. I know what I'm doing. PanGalacta is missing out."

Srinivas smiled. "You may be right, but it's too late now. You came up with that billion quickly and the contract is signed. I'm impressed."

"Thank you." Gwen wondered. This from a man who could throw twenty billion out a window and never even know it was gone.

"Anyway, I'm sorry to see you go. Your work has been outstanding."

"Thank you, Srinivas. You have always treated me well and I appreciate it."

A gentle tapping sound caused Gwen and the old man to turn toward the door. Nigellus Gardner stood in the doorway with an innocent smile. "Oh, I'm sorry. I could come back in a bit," he said with practiced modesty.

"Come on in, Nigellus. Gwen and I were just finishing up. She's placed the down payment on the spaceport and I've accepted her resignation."

"I see." Gardener glided into the office as if he was surprised. "You now start your new adventure. I wish you all the luck in the galaxy." He bowed his head slightly.

"Thank you, Nigellus. I'll need it, I'm sure." Gwen kept her rage under a lid, screwed tight. No satisfaction from her today. Plus she didn't believe in luck. "But now you both must excuse me. I have a lot of work to do."

"Of course." Srinivas shook Gwen's hand firmly. "It's been an honor. You'll notice I placed a bonus in your package."

"Well, thank you again." A bonus? That would come in handy soon no doubt. She turned to Nigellus. "This is it. Thank you for making me realize what I needed to do, Nigellus."

"You're quite welcome." Another pompous head bow.

Without another look, Gwen turned her back on her career and a CEO's office she had once coveted. But, she was happy to leave. As Gwen left the office she could hear Gardner. "Sir, if I may... the Melnyk-Saelim deal needs attention."

She felt sorry for Srinivas.

# 11

"SHE WENT FOR IT. I can't believe she went for it!" Nigellus Gardner clapped his hands and spun around. He had the lean and hungry look Shakespeare gave to Cassius.

"Yes, sir." The young man on the screen was less enthused than his superior, but he attentively watched the older man's movements.

"I have been waiting for this moment, Jonas." Indeed Nigellus had. He and Gwen had been on a collision course in PanGalacta for quite some time. However, she was gone now and no longer a threat.

"Of course, sir," the younger man agreed.

"She accepted an impossible task in a dead-end sector. How predictable."

"Certainly, sir. However, Ms. Davis has been very successful in her past endeavors."

"True." The thought lingered. She certainly was successful and smart. It would be foolish not to admit that.

But then again who was Gwendolyn Shepherd Davis anyway? Her father was an artist of some kind and her mother was a modestly successful academic.

Nigellus nearly verbalized his contempt. His parents were CEOs while he was still young. His father had gone on to be a planetary governor and an ambassador and his mother was currently serving in the cabinet for a third president. Besides, Ms. Davis only had one master's degree and one Ph.D. He passed his eyes over his luxurious office and all his plaques on the walls.

Achievement after achievement was chronicled there. Dual bachelor's degrees in macroeconomics and theoretical physics. Master's degrees in the philosophy of conceptual mathematics, operations research, computer science, business finance, and interplanetary relations. Not to mention a Jurius Doc and three PhDs in interplanetary monetary law, corporate law, and numerical analysis.

Nigellus loved this list and he went over it often, sometimes aloud to subordinates. He spared his employee this time, of course, the young man had heard it before.

"Well... " Nigellus started. "It would be a shame if she was not successful this time."

The young man on the screen nodded and the transmission terminated. The screen went black for only a fraction of a second and then began to show pleasant countryside scenes, some wholly unearthly.

Nigellus turned to one of the heavy laden bookcases. It was sprinkled with works from every historical period from the famous to the obscure. There were also a handful of books by his favorite author, himself.

He skipped his own *Gold from the Stars: The Legal and Business Ramifications of Four Theoretical Interstellar Commerce Monetary Models*. Brushed past Aristotle's *Nicomachean Ethics* and *The True Glories of Free Enterprise* Gwendolyn Shepherd Davis' doctoral dissertation. Then selected a leather-bound edition of Shakespeare's *Macbeth*.

Nigellus sat behind his darwood desk and opened the book. He read the inscription written in a powerful confident hand.

'To my son,

Never forget who you were born to be.

Your Father,

Governor Renfrow Sebastian Gardner, (ret.).'

# 12

JONAS CRANE spied the enormous snake without a moment to spare. Its camouflage was nearly perfect as it nestled in the rain forest's canopy. Without a move and the slightest beat of his heart, he ran computations and subroutines. After a split second, he was ready. He passed by the snake with an unearthly shimmer in his arms and legs. The snake moved but only a little and in a direction away from Jonas.

Jonas thought he had been a bit careless, so he doubled his vigilance. He tapped into more resources and pulled more bandwidth. It was tricky and this may be the hardest job he had ever done, but he knew what he was doing.

He continued his walk through the jungle. Dangers could lurk in any tree or under any rock. He placed every step as if a land mine may be under his foot, though he still managed to keep a fairly quick pace.

Jonas didn't like the look of the vine up ahead, so he halted his march. He began computations and processing. He looked up to see a giant leaf structure poised like a Venus flytrap. More computations, more processing. He plotted a route around the death trap.

This new route was better. He began to move more quickly. His form blurred now and then but it snapped back quickly. He would have made a strange sight, to say the least. His outfit was that of a medieval bard crossed with a 17th-century pirate. His leather belt and a bandoleer were filled with odd tools and a sword hung on his back.

He stopped. New course. He could see something up ahead. The rain forest opened in a clearing and he saw the foundation that looked like a Mayan pyramid. Computations. Processing.

In a moment he was there. The ancient stone structure rose above him. He could see that it was much higher than the canopy. The climb was arduous and Jonas took his time. Finally the top.

He could now see the entire jungle spread out around. Data flowed. Mapping. Mapping. Off to the north titanic snow-capped mountains stabbed up at the storm-ridden sky. His destination to be sure. But not today. He collected more data. More mapping.

His eyes rolled up and lids fluttered. The jungle, pyramid, and mountains hideously distorted. Jonas was now in complete darkness and alone in his own mind. The world around him returned as he slipped off the goggles and headset. The lights in the room ramped up, brighter and brighter. Computers, everywhere computers.

It had been a very productive day. He'd got closer to his goal and picked up some tidbits along the way. Every danger he passed and solution he discovered could be sold for a tidy profit. He'd hang on to a few in case he needed cash one day soon. A lot more work needed to be done, but right now he needed a drink.

# 13

"I THREW A BILLION into a quick flip real-estate deal out of Mongo Lai. It was risky, but the billion is now one point seven billion." Braeden seemed to be working on several other things as he spoke.

Gwen was impressed. "Excellent." Her eyes moved to a different screen. "Dave, how's everything on your end?"

"Perfectly fine. Recruiting is going well. Ms. Li is fulfilling all the requests for equipment..." Mercer trailed off a bit, recalling something. He looked like he hadn't slept in a couple of days. "Oh, any word on an uplifted animal interface?"

From a different screen, Bao spoke up. "Yes, there's been movement. I have a line on an octopus."

"Great." Mercer nodded. "At least it's not a dolphin."

"Do you have a problem with dolphins?" asked Gwen.

"Oh no. It's nothing. I was just thinking out loud." He seemed embarrassed.

Gwen could see he was exhausted. He worked non-stop when he was on. Kind of like she did in truth. He needed rest. So did she.

"That does bring up an issue I needed to discuss with Mr. Foster." Bao shifted her gaze. "I'll need several hundred million in outer system ducats. A seller is insisting."

"They won't take unions? It really is a different world on the rim, isn't it?" Braeden shook his head.

"Is there a problem with acquiring ducats?" Gwen didn't want anything to stand in her way.

"No, not at all." Braeden's confidence was evident and Bao nodded.

Gwen leaned back in her chair. "Ridley and Edison, I'm sorry. I've kind of neglected you two. How do things stand?"

Ridley spoke up first. "No worries. Everything is going well. There are always flight controllers looking for work."

"Fine here. I think Ms. Li found almost everything we needed quicker than I thought possible. My core engineering team in place. We're ready to hit the ground and get our hands on the spaceport." Edison's smile was engaging.

"Fantastic work." Gwen was ready to get the spaceport as well, but there was more work to be done before that could happen. "I'm still putting together a board of directors. I don't have good leads for the chief of security or the chief medical officer. I contacted several candidates, but they weren't interested."

"I could help with the chief of security," Braeden spoke up.

Gwen nodded.

"Would it be okay if I reached out to a chief medical officer candidate?" Ridley seemed a bit unsure of himself.

"Of course." Gwen wanted her team to be active. She leaned forward in her chair and thought for a brief moment.

The nucleus of Gwen's team blinked at her from five different screens. It had been a feat to get them all on one call together, but here they were. Experts in all their chosen fields and Gwen was proud to work with them.

Gwen's office was dark and only illuminated by the myriad of screens around her. It was a little past three AM her time and she had been working solid for sixteen hours.

"Thank you all for the hard work. Everything is coming together. Stay in communication."

The faces on the screens nodded and one by one they were replaced by pictures of Gwen's husband and daughters.

Gwen rubbed her eyes. Time for two hours of sleep.

# 14

THE BLAST CATAPULTED Ari Frost off the ground. He crashed into the hard burgundy soil with a heavy groan, rolled, and came up with his rifle ready. The viewfinder in the rifle scope zoomed in and out as Ari searched the small hillock.

A series of beeps and the viewfinder zoomed in on a man partially camouflaged in the feathery brown scrub grass on the faraway hill. Ari could see the soldier reloading a mortar. A Mark-1015 Ulysses ProTech mortar, the pre-Bug War model, with a Titan Fairtex range assist. No wonder it had missed. They were notoriously inaccurate.

A yellow triangle appeared in Ari's scope. It rotated around a man who was furiously locking another shell into place. The triangle stopped rotating and flashed red. Ari squeezed the trigger twice.

Two loping bullets screamed in a high arc out of his rifle. The first spat out thousands of tiny needles that descended in an umbrella-shaped cloud. The soldier and two previously unseen companions began to wriggle like fish on hooks. The needle-drones sank through their body armor into their flesh. Electric charges and micro-explosions racked their bodies. The second round burrowed into the ground near the mortar then exploded with enough force to heave up large clumps of earth.

Ari's scope indicated three kills and no remaining life signs. He quickly lowered his rifle and found cover behind a rock formation.

Dillon was playing a dangerous game and Ari was tired of it. Even though their unit had superior weapons and training, using men as bait was risky and uncalled for. But here they were.

Dillon called the shots and the strategy had worked so far, but this had been a close call. Too close for Ari's liking since it had been his skin on the line for the last week. Why was Dillon doing this? There were other strategies, other tactics. A lack of imagination is all.

Ari spun and raised his rifle above the rock formation. Through the scope, he surveyed the havoc he'd wrought. That Ulysses ProTech wouldn't hurt anyone ever again. Then he moved the scope to view the distant forest line behind the hill, if it could be called a forest. The trees, as they were called, were thorny twisted things with looping vines and sail-like plumes that gave off great clouds of pollen in the breeze.

Something moved in the forest. His scope tried to focus. No clear lock, but the scanner showed metal. Most likely tanks creeping through the thorny forest. Ari pressed a button on his rifle. An orange outline highlighted the trees. Ari pressed another button.

Fire rained from the heavens. The brambly trees with their twisted vines went up in a roaring conflagration. The greedy flames leaped up the giant sails, consuming them to nothingness. So intense was the heat that even the pollen clouds caught fire sending tiny fireworks into the sky.

One last sweep with his scope. No life signs. Ari sat back down behind the rock formation and pinged his marker beacon. The transport would be here in nearly an instant to retrieve him.

Something on the rock formation caught his eye. He noticed a pattern and followed the lines with his eyes. The fossilized outline of some three-toed bird-like creature. Did it have a name? How old was it?

The transport whooshed next to him. The door unfolded and the interior welcomed him. He crawled inside and the door folded closed. He eased into the reclined chair. He didn't have to do a thing, the transport knew where to go and the rest of his unit would move in on his position to cover the evac.

"Good work, Frost," came a confident professional voice.

"Thank you, sir." Ari relaxed.

With his right hand, he pulled a small cable out of his uniform's left shoulder and plugged it into a jack on the chair. The screen in the transport blinked to life; the battlefield and his handiwork. Tompkins, Xi, Riberio moving toward the forest. Plus indicators.

He had received several messages. Two were junk, one was from his sister; he'd have to write her later.

The last message was strange. It read: "Mr. Frost, a friend recommended you for a job. Please reach out as soon as possible for more information. Braeden Foster."

# 15

"TWO HUNDRED METRIC tons of triglass, five hundred thousand metric tons of quallcrete, three hundred thousand metric tons of zinsteel, thirty thousand meters of dekcable, twelve thousand Int-Teq microprocessors, and ten thousand meters of mirlon-filament cable have all been routed to a holding warehouse on Bolivar. The purchase of an octopus named Septimus was completed. Mr. Foster came through with the outer system ducats as well as the PhaneCoin and Maxum credits that were needed for other purchases."

Bao's voice was distorted, but Gwen heard it all. Gwen gazed at the screen and watched Bao's face. What a good hire this one was. "Thank you, Bao. These supplies along with the others will give us an excellent start."

"It's my pleasure. I hope I didn't bore you with the details."

"No, no. It's exactly what I wanted to hear. But, I should let you go. Make sure you take a break."

"Yes, ma'am." Bao's smiling face blinked out and became a picture of Gwen's daughters in a pile of leaves.

Gwen leaned back and sighed. Hands reached around her shoulders and began to squeeze. She sighed again.

"You don't have to do that," Gwen said without looking behind her.

"I want to," Liam answered.

"Okay, rub away." Gwen relaxed as her husband gently rubbed her shoulders.

"You're pushing yourself too hard."

"Maybe. There's still so much to be done. I need more team members and a lawyer. I've already contacted four who turned me down..."

Liam laughed.

"All right, I'm pushing too hard." She insisted on knowing about every purchase, but she got lost in the weeds. Bao and Braeden were pros. They took care of everything. She needed to search for investors and a good lawyer.

Liam's fingers rolled away some stress.

"I made you dinner. Come eat with me." Liam continued to kneed her shoulders.

"Dinner? It's 1:57 am."

"So? You haven't eaten, have you?"

Gwen's stomach reminded her she hadn't eaten in hours.

"Come on." Liam nudged her and then leaned down and kissed her on the cheek.

"Dinner does sound good."

# 16

JONAS CRANE rubbed the cooling salve on his blistered temple. An extremely close call had burned his face and addled his wits. Everything was good though.

He threw the security bots off his trail. A Cyber-Action Team would most likely raid an abandoned building on Sturgis in the next few hours, but they wouldn't find a trace of evidence linking him to the crime. He'd have to lay low for a few days until the salve worked its magic. Besides, he could use a filter on any communications and no one would be the wiser.

The screen in front of him flashed 'COMPILING' over and over again. He'd scored a lot of data this run. Lots of data. He'd need it too. He needed to upgrade his hardware after the burn incident. Several pieces would sell for quite a lot.

Right now he'd shake the fog out of his brain. He'd set up the data auctions later. He checked the time. He'd been in for six hours. Time for a break. Mr. Gardener was getting his money's worth from this job.

# 17

"LADIES AND GENTLEMEN, Redcliff Spaceport." Gwen paused for effect. She looked the six other people in the room in the eye and then moved her gaze to the six on screens. This was the kicker; she hoped to impress her audience.

In the center of the conference room a holographic image appeared. A massive river poured over a crescent cliff. The water fell nearly three thousand meters. Intertwined among the river and the cliff was a spaceport. Docking bays dotted the sheer red cliff. In the center of the river at the top of the falls, a large tower built on a rock formation reached a thousand meters into the sky.

"Located on the planet Erebus in the Nindira Rim sector, Redcliff Spaceport has sat empty since the end of the AI War. The planet itself is sparsely populated with two cities of consequence – Newcastle, the capital, and Freetown.

"However, the sector is growing as more planets open up and settlers push farther out. With its location, Redcliff Spaceport is primed to become the hub of the sector. Currently, ships operating in the vicinity are forced to land on the raw surface of most planets. As you know, this increases the risk of crashes and the loss of life. A fully-equipped spaceport changes the entire landscape of the sector."

Gwen read the faces of her audience. All of them seasoned businessmen and women, all of them billionaires with money to invest. "Now, who wants a piece of the action?" Gwen smiled.

A smile greeted her. "Gwen, if I may?" came a voice from one of the faces on a screen. The woman was in her mid-sixties with silver hair pulled back in a bun.

"Of course," Gwen acknowledged her.

"After all this time, are you sure someone else hasn't set up shop there?"

"Yes, the local authorities patrol the area occasionally and report no squatters. However, we are operating under the assumption that the site has been, let's say, mined for materials in the past. We have security and engineering teams gearing up. Once they arrive, they will conduct full inspections."

"It's all very impressive." A man who looked to be about eighty said. He sat in the conference room only a few scant meters from Gwen. "I'd like to take a closer look at some of your numbers so far."

"Of course, I've provided an information packet. You should have all received it. Also, there's no rush. I'll reach out to all after you've had a chance to think about it." She was being polite. She needed investors today, but she knew she couldn't rush them into any decisions anyway.

Another gentleman spoke up. Gwen didn't know him well. Chow was the name and he stood out from the others as he was incredibly young to be a billionaire. "What about the pirate situation in the sector?" His voice was casual and he watched Gwen closely.

Gwen measured the silent reactions of others in the audience. She knew this question was coming. "It is concerning, Mr. Chow. However, I'm addressing that and will have an update soon. Rest assured, I'm doing everything in my power to ensure the safety and success of this venture."

# 18

THE CAFE HUMMED around Gwen. A fresh breeze blew. The smell of freshly baked bread and coffee flowed with it. Dishes tinkled. People chattered. A million things swirled through Gwen's mind. Building supplies, hiring staff and workers, permits, more permits, investors, structuring the corporation, money, more money... And her host was telling her about tea.

"This particular variation contains delicate after notes of a sweet nut only found on Narvik Poord." The practically handsome man cradled a teacup and took a sip. His eyelids fluttered. He let out a deep breath. "Over a hundred different teas are blended in a process that takes two years to complete." He gingerly placed the cup on its saucer. "But... you didn't come here to discuss tea."

No, she had not, thought Gwen. However, she smiled warmly. "It's fascinating."

The man smiled back. "You humor me. I'm used to it, though. My colleagues are always teasing me about how every Thursday morning I jaunt off to Vienna for a cup of tea. But enough... I presented your report to the joint chiefs and they were impressed."

Gwen inwardly relaxed.

The man continued. "They agree. Their efforts in the sector have been hampered by not having a permanent base. They have also agreed to lease a portion of the spaceport for a sector command and a fighter wing base."

Gwen stayed calm. This was the best news in weeks.

The man sipped his tea. "However, they have very specific specifications for the facilities they require, and they've asked that sector commander Admiral Peele be given a seat on the board."

Gwen only thought for a nanosecond. "I completely understand. Absolutely doable."

"Fantastic." The man said as he sipped his tea. "I'll pass along your agreement and put you in touch with all the right people. Is there anything else I can do for you?"

"No, but I'll take a cup of that tea now."

"Excellent." Then, over his shoulder, "A cup of tea for Ms. Davis."

A young waiter bolted into action with a crisp, "Yes, Senator."

The senator looked back at Gwen. "Gwen, when are you going to run for office?"

Gwen smiled. "Too much on my plate at the moment, but who knows what the future holds."

# 19

DRAKE PENDLETON CHOW brushed his mind clear. Companies and money. Lots of thoughts about money. Deals gone wrong and deals gone right. The fight with his girlfriend. His father's death. His younger brother's drug problem. All swept away and tucked into a quiet deep place.

Birds chirped and the manicured green rolled out before him. He took a deep breath. He focused all his attention on the tiny white ball. The club felt good in his hands. It should. It cost him fifty thousand unions. Concentrating on his angles, he pulled the club back. Chow's torso blurred and the little white ball flew into the air and out of sight. He settled back and waited. A phantom-like number floated in midair '245 meters.' He nodded with satisfaction.

He turned his head and the entire golf course disappeared. He stood now in a well-appointed office. Several large autographed posters of bands hung on the walls. The one of the Himalayan Monkey Twisters was worth more than three times the golf club. He handed the golden driver to a woman who stood nearby. She raced off with it and disappeared through a door.

Chow moved quickly to his desk. The driving session helped him think. Now, he would act. He pressed a button on his computer. "Yes, sir?" came a lovely voice.

"Harper, send a message to Ms. Davis. Ask her on what terms would she accept a billion investment."

"Of course, sir. Also, a few minutes ago you received a message from

Ms. Davis. It said the deal with the government went through."

Ah, his instincts had been right again. "Excellent. Thank you, Harper..." He paused. His instincts screamed at him.

"Yes, sir?" The voice wondered if the conversation was over.

"Oh yes. Call Mr. Faraday and put him through to my screen."

"Of course, sir."

Chow sat behind his desk. Yes, he was right about this too. Mr. Faraday should be informed.

# 20

THE GLOWING SNOWSHOES produced an electronic hissing sound upon contact with the pseudo-snow. Computations. Processing. Collecting data. This session had been a long one, but Jonas Crane finally crested the mountain. His mind felt like it had been dragged over the Dagger Desert of Satara Blud. Nevertheless, his goal had been reached.

Snow blew in his face. He shivered and pulled the long dark coat tighter around him. Several boulders lay ahead of him. He halted. Computations. Processing. Collecting data. From behind the boulders arose six dark figures. They fanned out and surrounded him.

A seventh figure shimmered into existence. Heavily mantled with a great cloak, shrouded by mist, it slowly approached Jonas. Computations. Processing. Collecting data. Jonas was ready for anything.

The figure croaked. "You've come a long way." Jonas raised a hand. Pulsating lines like a chain link fence appeared around the top of the mountain. The hooded figure nodded. "Even more security. Excellent," it hissed.

"I have a job. A spaceport project in the Nindira Rim sector needs to fail." Jonas' mouth didn't move. It wasn't even his face.

"I lack equipment and funds. The GU has hit us hard in the Nindira Rim sector."

"Understood. All can be arranged." An ethereal book of numbers appeared next to Jonas. The figure gasped. The object proved Jonas had enough money to make the job worth it.

"Very well. We are your servants." The figure bowed slightly.

"Now, let's get to work. We haven't much time." Jonas was proud of his work.

# 21

"Everything's arranged. Mr. Frost's security team and Mr. Botani's engineering teams will be the first on the ground. Their priority is to make the site livable and safe. Approximately one week later, I and the rest of the senior staff will touch down." Exhaustion weighed on Gwen's mind like a net holding a diver under the sea.

Yet, she fought through it. She was close. Close to seeing the spaceport. Close to realizing this dream. Too close to give up now. "Everyone clear on their assignments and travel arrangements?"

All the faces on the screens nodded back to her. Everyone was ready. This was the time.

"Very good. If anything changes, let me know immediately. I'll see some of you very soon and, Ari and Edison, we all look forward to meeting you at the spaceport." More nods as Gwen ended the meeting.

Here she was. This whole spaceport business was about to get real. But she wanted it more than ever. To get her feet there and to see it and to get it operational again. That was her focus.

She let those thoughts free her mind from the fatigue. Four-twelve AM, but she didn't want to go to bed. Plus Liam was sound asleep and she didn't want to disturb him. She crept out of the office and down the stairs to the kitchen.

She was hungrier than she realized. Pistachio butter toast would fill the spot. Her excitement ebbed. Her leaving in a few days did mean she would travel to the spaceport but it also meant she would be leaving Liam behind. He had to finish up a lot of work before he could relocate to the spaceport.

What about their daughters? She'd be so far away from them. They were grown and off living their own lives. She'd be so far away. What if they needed her?

The first bite of the warm pistachio toast refreshed her. No time for second-guessing now. Her daughters and Liam would be fine. All agreed she should do this.

"Go to bed," came a sleep-filled voice. Gwen smiled as Liam stumbled into the kitchen.

"I didn't wake you, did I?"

"No, just thirsty." He filled a glass with water.

"Good."

"Go to bed." Liam turned to leave the kitchen after gulping.

Gwen couldn't help but smile again. "I'll be right up."

Liam exited with a sleepy thumbs up. Gwen enjoyed the rest of her toast and steeled herself for the adventure ahead.

# PART 2:
# REBUILDING

Rebuild rebuilding
How do you rebuild the lost?
One brick at a time

- The Poet Loam

# 1

As she stepped out of the elevator, Gwen thought the bridge of the liner *Emperor of India* was well organized. She found Captain Ellen Krause to be an excellent host for the journey.

"Ah, Ms. Davis." The captain turned at the sound of the elevator doors. "Welcome to the bridge. I thought you would enjoy the approach to Erebus."

"Absolutely. Thank you for the invitation." She could see data being displayed on the main screen, but couldn't see the planet. "How long until we arrive?"

"About thirty minutes." The captain said after glancing at a small screen near the command chair. "We'll be able to put the planet on screen in just a minute or two."

Gwen stepped forward and stood by the captain's side. The main screen changed to show a computer-generated model of the star system and the ship's location. Suddenly several more indicators appeared. The smaller red shapes raced toward the *Emperor of India*'s large yellow icon.

"Inbound craft!" Someone on the bridge yelled.

"Scan them," the captain responded.

"On it," came a voice from one of the bridge officers. "Fighter craft. Three, no seven, no twelve. All on an intercept course. Now I'm reading a destroyer class ship. On screen." The main viewer changed. Small fighter craft hurled through space and the outline of a larger ship bared down and moved into view.

"Oh my god." Gwen's chest tightened.

"Alert. All stations. Alert. We are under attack. Prepare defensive measures. Sound general quarters." The captain barked orders and her crew snapped to. "Send a distress call on all frequencies."

"Aye, Captain," came a reply.

Pirates. Not now, not this. All her people. Gwen had put them all in terrible danger. She needed to get to the spaceport. "Can you fight them off?" Gwen asked the captain.

"No, we only have minimal defensive capabilities. We'll try to get to the planet." The captain switched her attention. "Helm increase speed toward Erebus."

"Aye, aye," another voice.

Gwen had never been in combat; never even a physical fight. This was new and terrifying. She watched the fighter craft scream closer. Energy bolts.

An ear-splitting boom. The massive liner lurched. Gwen fell in complete darkness. Screaming. The smell of smoke. Disorientation.

"Emergency lights!" someone yelled close, yet far away from Gwen. Dim lights clicked on with a wheezing sound.

Gwen found herself on her hands and knees. An acrid odor of burning wires filled her nose and turned her stomach. Smoke clawed at her throat like a wild Spear-cat. Something warm was on her face. It filled her eyebrow and lashes on the right side and ran down her cheek. Blood.

"Damage report," shouted the captain, "and get this smoke out of here!"

"Direct hit. Defensive shields are down."

Gwen summoned her strength and rose to her feet. She wiped her eye with her sleeve. It came back stained dark red. This was when she saw the dead body; a bridge officer cast in such a position he could only be dead. Handsome and young, so young. About the same age as Alexandra.

The ship shuddered. "Captain, we're being hailed. The attackers are demanding our surrender."

Gwen looked at Captain Krause. She could see the anguish in her face. More alarms went off. More shaking. Sparks flew from a console.

Captain Krause began slowly and half to herself at first, "Very well. Inform them we surren—"

"Captain!" cut in a crew member. "A new group of signals dropping out of slipspace."

"Identify." The captain demanded.

"GU cruiser *Apollo*. They are launching fighters. The *Apollo* is firing on the destroyer."

Gwen's heart leaped.

"Belay that surrender order," cried the captain.

"With pleasure."

Gwen watched as the tide of the battle turned and it turned quickly. The Galactic Union fighters closed and engaged the hostile fighters. The pirate fighters had no choice but to abandon the attack on the *Emperor of India* and fight for their lives.

The *Apollo* rained fire on the pirate destroyer. Yet the destroyer took only minimal damage. It maneuvered and fled the system. The *Apollo* did not give chase. Instead, it turned and supported its fighters. Then it was over. So fast.

"The commander of the *Apollo* is hailing." Gwen thought the voice sounded far away. Fog permeated her thinking and the young man's face was still before her eyes.

"On screen," Krause acknowledged.

The main screen displayed the face of a man about forty years of age in a crisp uniform. His dark hair was flecked with gray. "I'm Captain Brady Pratt of the *USS Apollo*. What's your situation, Captain?"

"I'm Captain Krause. Major engine damage. We'll have to shut them down." Krause glanced at the screen near her chair. "Injury reports are just coming in. At least several dead, including my navigator. Thank you, Captain Pratt. You saved us all."

"You're welcome, Captain. I'm sorry about your crewman. We picked up your distress signal right before the pirates started jamming comms. We were headed here as well. We can tow you to Erebus. Is that your destination?"

"Yes, sir. That would be appreciated. You're headed to Erebus?"

"Yes, we have business there."

Gwen fought her way back to the present. Does the GU ship have business on Erebus? Could it be? Unsure of the etiquette on space ship communications she hesitated, but then spoke up.

"Captain Krause, please excuse me. Captain Pratt, is your mission to drop personnel and equipment off at Redcliff Spaceport?"

"Why, yes. And who may you be?"

"I'm Gwendolyn Shepherd Davis, the new owner of the spaceport."

"Ah, I've been looking forward to meeting you. Sorry it was under these circumstances." Pratt eyed her. "You've been injured."

"I'm fine. Thank you so much for saving us." Gwen smiled.

Pratt nodded. "I look forward to meeting you on the surface. We have much to discuss." Captain Pratt looked down and then up. "Captain Krause, cut all power to your engines. We're moving into towing position."

"Aye, Captain Pratt. Cutting all power. Ready to be towed."

With such an eventful arrival, Gwen wondered how Frost and Edison fared on the surface.

# 2

EDISON'S FIRST WEEK on Erebus was a whirlwind. Hundreds, if not thousands, of decisions. His team was doing a great job, but the task was Herculean. So much was being thrown at him so fast. He was ready and had detailed plans, but the speed at which he needed to work was unrelenting. He hadn't slept in twenty-eight hours.

He marched past the techs and the construction drones. The rows of prefab housing went up fast along the edge of the great landing pad just as they were designed to of course. They only had their drop ship here for a week. The prefab housing would fill the gap between when the ship left and the spaceport could be occupied. If there was a gap. He was pushing hard to have the spaceport ready.

However, his first glances told him to be patient. The spaceport was a wreck. The security had moved through several sections and hadn't found any squatters or death traps yet, but there was still time.

Power. That was the main concern. Power. If he could restore power to the station, climate control, air, water, food would all fall like dominoes. He needed to see the core and the AI Well. Captain Frost wouldn't allow it. Security teams still needed to sweep the areas and the spaceport was huge after all. He'd get there soon though.

He stopped near the last prefab housing unit and looked out in the desert-like scrubland. He wished he could take his helmet off, but the waterfall made that impossible. The great river snaked its way back to an almost imperceptible mountain range at the misty horizon. The plants along the river banks had strange funnel-like leaves. Vividly yellow birds flitted among the shoots. Wait... Was something big moving out there?

He zoomed in with his helmet's visor. Yes. Slinking around some bushes. That had to be an Erebus wolf, although, despite its name, it was actually some kind of feline. He watched it disappear in the spongy funnel leaves near the river.

Home. Well, at least for a while. Maybe he'd meet someone and they could take a trip to see those mountains. He could retrofit a quadsport with some camping gear and a—

A hand on Edison's shoulder shattered his daydream. It was one of his senior techs. She motioned to him. Oh, he had turned off his helmet comm. He switched it on.

"Mr. Botani?" the young feminine voice asked.

"Yes, Ms. Laine?"

"Captain Frost is trying to reach you. Ms. Davis' ship was attacked en route and is being towed in. She was injured."

"Oh my god."

# 3

THE GREAT CRESCENT CLIFF with the thundering waterfall unfolded beneath her. Her heart quickened. Most of the land she could see from this altitude belonged to her. Unbelievable, yet here she was. It was also unbelievable that three of her people were dead. A sector overrun with pirates... Was she mad for bringing everyone out here?

Gwen could see the ship on the giant landing pad and the rows of prefab housing. The people were specks, barely visible. As the shuttle descended, the full extent of the work could be seen. Her people had been busy.

"Before you land, swing around. I'd like to see the cliff face." Gwen asked the pilot. She touched the bandage on her forehead. Oh, the doctor said don't fiddle with it.

"Will do, ma'am." The pilot altered course and the craft performed a slow half-circle past the control tower and out over the waterfall far below.

Now Gwen could see the plunging water clearly and the massive bubbling cauldron it created at the base of the cliff. The pilot maneuvered the shuttle and they dropped below the rim of the cliff.

The arms of the cliff spread out like the wings of a roc. Different-sized holes marked the red cliff face like the cliff dwellings on Oregalus. Landing bays all of them. Tangled wires and cables hung limp in some. Gigantic beams plunged out of the ceiling or the floor in others. Edison and his team had their work cut out for them. They all did.

Yet, Gwen could picture ships coming and going. Hundreds, thousands maybe. And people, too. From all over the Galactic Union and more. And at the center, Redcliff Spaceport.

"Very good. Take us up." She was ready to get to work.

# 4

ARI FROST switched on the gun barrel light and pointed it through a hole in the hull. It illuminated the interior of the ship. It had been spotted on the first survey pass of the spaceport nine days ago, but this was the first chance he'd got to explore it.

It looked as though the pilot had tried to land in one of the docking bays, but couldn't make it for some reason and ended up crashed in the river valley. Probably scavengers looking for parts or something. They'd know soon enough. Edison had loaned him a technician to help see if the computers on board had any clues.

He moved inside cautiously and waved several other security officers in behind him. The corridors were empty and there were no signs of life. He motioned. "Jenkins and Sato, engine room. Thompson and Lyons, with me."

He picked his way through the dim hallways and emerged in the cockpit or what was left of it. The crash had not been kind and the cockpit was severely damaged. Then he saw them. Two badly decomposed bodies. He hit his comm. "Frost to base, have a medical team sent to the crash site. I've found two bodies and I need forensics."

"Understood, Captain Frost."

Ari noticed something. He looked closer. Next to the bodies were pieces of twine tied like hearts. A memorial? Someone survived the crash?

"Captain Frost." His comm blared.

"Yes."

"The wreck is clear. Nothing's alive in here."

"Understood. Have the technician brought in to start work on the computers."

"Yes, sir. Jenkins out."

Ari considered the twine hearts once again. If someone survived the crash, where would they be? He looked up through the smashed triglass cockpit windows. The spaceport loomed above him on the massive cliff.

# 5

LULONI HEARD THEM coming and hid. She had known they were here for a week or more. She didn't worry at first, but it was obvious that they were searching every room in the spaceport. Now, they were on top of her. They'd find her favorite room in a few moments. She pressed her body as far as it could go into the cubby hole.

"Sir, someone lives here." She couldn't see them because of the angle, but she heard a voice. It was a woman and she spoke Standard English. Luloni was rusty with Standard English, but she understood.

"It's still occupied by the look." This was a man's voice. He spoke in Standard English too. She wished they were speaking Outer System English or even Fringese.

"Hello? Is anyone here? We are not here to hurt you. We want to help you." It was the man speaking. Oh, by the free lords Luloni wanted help, but her arms shook and her lips trembled. She'd be in so much trouble, wouldn't she?

"We're friends. We want to help you." It was the woman and she spoke in Outer System English. Luloni was so hungry. She needed help.

"I'm here, but I'm scared." It seemed to her as if someone else spoke. But it was her voice. A voice she hadn't used in a year or more.

"It's okay. You can come out." The woman said. Luloni gathered her courage. She crept out from her hiding place. She looked around the corner into the room. A lightning crack of fear. Hide! Hide! She pulled back, trembling.

"No, no. It's okay," came the friendly woman's voice. "Please don't be afraid. We're here to help."

"Guns. You have guns." Luloni knew something about guns. Well, a lot actually. None of it good. She had seen her father use guns on people. She hated those memories.

"I'm sorry. We're a security team. Listen. We'll put them down."

Luloni heard sounds as if something was placed on the ground. She peeked out. The woman and the man had placed their guns on the ground. They were standing with their hands open and arms wide. They wore tactical gear and body armor. She had seen that before too.

She stepped out in front of the two. The woman smiled. "You're okay. We're friends."

Luloni shivered, but she nodded. "I need food."

"Of course you do, sweetheart. Everything will be alright. I'm going to talk into my comm." The woman moved her hand slowly toward her mouth. "Bravo Team to Base."

"Base, go ahead."

"Inform Captain Frost we found an individual. Please have a medical team and some hot food ready. Over."

"Understood. Base out."

The woman's smile was disarming. Luloni smiled back. Hot food sounded perfect.

# 6

As soon as Gwen heard the news she cut her tour of the spaceport short. Now, she stood in a hurriedly-erected medical tent on the large landing pad. Dr. Roseline Pierre and several others buzzed around. Sitting in front of her was a thin, filthy, terrified waif of a girl dressed in rags and chewing on a warm Barling cake.

"My name is Gwen. I'm in charge here. Do you mind if I ask you a few questions?"

The girl shook her head and licked cream filling like she was starving. Probably was. Gwen smiled. On second thought, a different tactic. "Do you want to know something? I have four daughters. The youngest is, I'd say about two or three years older than you."

The girl looked at her. "I'm fifteen."

"Ah, then she's three years older than you. The security team said your name is Luloni."

"Yes."

Gwen thought the girl was hesitating. Translating? The security said she responded to Outer System English. Sadly, Gwen didn't know it. In addition to Standard English, she spoke French, German, Yoruba, a bit of Hausa, and she could get by in Core Speak. But she had never focused on the outer languages. Why? Probably some sort of prejudice against the people on the rim. That needed to change, especially since she was going to live here.

"They also said you and your family crashed here a year ago. The ship down at the base of the waterfall."

"Yes."

"Only you survived, right?"

The girl nodded this time. Profound sadness stretched across her dirty, tired face. Gwen wanted to hug her like she was one of her daughters, but of course, she refrained.

"I'm so sorry, Luloni." Gwen tried to meet the girl's eyes. Luloni looked down and worked on the cake more. Gwen glanced at the doctor and the nurses.

"Will I be arrested now?" The girl's voice was barely above a whisper, yet the words struck Gwen like a thunderclap.

"Arrested? Honey, no. Why? Why would we arrest you?"

"My parents stole the ship."

Gwen shook off the shock that this poor child thought she would be arrested. "They did? Even if that's true, we would not arrest you. You're a child. You're not responsible for any crimes they may have committed." Luloni looked confused. She probably spoke too fast. Gwen knelt and touched Luloni's knees. "You are not in trouble. You will not be arrested."

Luloni nodded. *She understands, good.*

Gwen looked to Dr. Pierre. "Is she okay?"

"Yes, remarkably healthy. All things considered. She's malnourished and has lice. The next steps are a bath, lice treatment, vitamins, more food, and a good night's sleep in safety."

Gwen looked back to Luloni. "Does all that sound good?" Luloni nodded vigorously.

"Good," said Gwen as she stood up. "I have to go now. You'll be well cared for. I'll come back and see you soon."

Luloni munched more of the cake. Gwen turned and left the tent. Buying a spaceport came with more responsibilities than she ever thought.

# 7

"THAT WAS GREAT timing, Dr. Mercer."

An electric hum echoed throughout the spaceport and lights flickered on at the exact moment David Mercer entered the power room. "It was, Mr. Botani. But please, you can call me Dave."

"Well, then, I'm Edison." The youthful engineer hopped down from a ladder and approached Mercer.

David greeted him with a handshake but was soon distracted. The power room buzzed with life. Technicians scurried between rows of pulsating cylinders. "Excellent work by the way. You were able to restore power quickly."

David could tell Edison loved the praise. "Thank you. I planned for the worst-case scenario, but fortunately, it wasn't anywhere near that. The main power cables were cut and the Pierson Regulator was missing all according to the standard corporate procedure."

"No looting?"

"Oh, it had been looted. Lots of small pieces were taken. I accounted for that when bringing spare parts."

David nodded. "Good job. What do you have control over now?"

"Most of the basic environmental systems. I need to check with my teams, but that's where we are at."

David liked this engineer. "I'll let you get back to work soon, but first I'd like to see the AI Well."

"Of course, right this way."

Edison led David on a winding path through the cylinders until they arrived at a set of doors in the chamber's east wall. Edison went to an open control panel and pulled the manual overdrive lever. The doors opened.

"I'll get the lights. I've only seen it with flashlights until now." Edison fiddled with the panel.

David stepped up and looked inside. Lights blinked and flickered on. He had only seen pictures of AI Wells up until now. It was huge and it yawned before him. Hundreds of thousands, millions of wires and cables hung lifeless like vines from the forest canopies on Blackwelder.

He cautiously entered and realized he stood on an observation deck. It ringed the AI Well and looked quite sturdy.

*Oh my god.* David was in awe. Nightmare weavers had all the materials they needed here. All the stories from the AI War came flooding back to him. The history he had read. Things his grandparents told him. Terrifying machines without empathy or emotion burning and devastating worlds. But humans won. Here was proof of that.

"What are the dimensions?" David's voice was quiet like he was in a church or a tomb.

"One hundred forty-two meters across. Half a kilometer up and a little more than one kilometer down." Edison stepped up beside him.

"I read about it. Redcliff AI Designate 4636570-676733-121 or 'Clifford' as christened by the spaceport's original crew." David gaped.

"Did it go crazy?"

"No, it never showed any signs of the AI Madness. However, it was still sentenced to death along with all other AI." David sometimes dreamed of AI. He could build one, he knew could, and that frightened him.

"There were good reasons they all had to go."

"True, but what a tragedy it turned into."

"More than forty billion lives lost. One of the worst tragedies."

And the countless AIs that were in everything from spaceports to ships to watches. Did he just equate human lives with AI lives? David pulled himself out of the past and questions of ethics. "Where were you thinking of putting the uplifted animal interface?"

"Over there." Edison pointed to a section of the observation deck that bulged out into a half-circle. "There's plenty of room for the tank and all the connections are nearby."

David appraised the location. "Good, that will work perfectly." David knew he'd spend a lot of time in this room.

# 8

*How am I ever going to get work done with a view like this?* Gwen wondered as she paced slowly around what was to be her office. The clear dome at the very top of the tower afforded a three hundred sixty-degree view of the surrounding landscape.

To the south, the river plunged into the valley and became a writhing twisted thing until it vanished out of view in the maze of rocky canyons. To the north, the river weaved through the arid plains like a colossal serpent until it disappeared out of sight in the misty mountain range looked no larger than a row of children's teeth. To the east and west first, one could see the several gigantic landing pads and then the plains stretched until the curvature of Erebus stole them away.

Footsteps interrupted her thoughts. Several people came up the spiral staircase in the middle of the room from Control and Command. Braeden Foster was leading two other individuals – a woman dressed in a smart business suit and a man in a crisp GU officer's uniform.

Gwen had been briefed on them and was expecting to meet them later today. Something had changed.

"Ms. Davis, Langley Khoroushi, governmental liaison, and Commander Bellamy Cooper, commanding officer of the spaceport detachment," Braeden stated quickly.

"It's a pleasure, but earlier than expected." Gwen didn't want another problem to deal with, but problems were the norm these days.

"Yes, Ms. Davis." Langley's voice was confident. "Something has changed."

"Captain Pratt is certain that the pirates in this sector are receiving aid or financing on a scale we haven't seen before." The Commander's voice was powerful, deep, and touched with a hint of a Porus 2 accent or at least that's what Gwen assumed.

"What evidence does he have?" Pirates. The absolute last thing Gwen wished she had to deal with.

"Nothing direct as yet. However, the rate at which the pirates are resupplying is highly suspicious," added Langley.

"Yes," continued Commander Cooper. "The *Apollo* has destroyed several ships and bases in the sector over the last year. Normally, that would reduce pirate activity substantially yet they seem to be growing stronger."

Gwen rolled this information over in her head. Well-funded murderous pirates? A spaceport that was falling apart? Thousands of people depending on her? No sense complaining. "I see. What are Captain Pratt's recommendations?"

"Speed up the fighter wing's relocation to the base and shift priorities to defensive systems," the commander answered. "Also, Captain Pratt has requested permission to keep the *Apollo* in the area longer than was scheduled."

All these precautions were sensible, Gwen thought. "Very well. I'll bring up defensive systems with the engineering and technology teams."

There were some thanks, agreements, pleasantries, and then Foster led Khoroushi and Cooper back down the stairs. Gwen looked out over the spaceport. She was helpless when it came to pirates. She hated that feeling. But there was something she could do.

# 9

GOODLUCK OMASI was a big man who loved small comforts. He loved his tiny Neo-Tokyo Post-Re-constructionist bungalow. Its lines were perfect and serene. He loved his tiny Malaysian wife. Her lines were perfect too.

He loved the smell of the Alrusian coffee blend that filled the tiny kitchen every morning. He loved the little breakfast nook where he and his wife would eat before she went off to work. He loved the tiny kiss his wife gave his cheek as she left. He loved the quiet house during the day.

He would sit in the sun and read and read and read. He'd just completed a wide survey of the western genre. He read the greats like Grey, L'Amour, and Kelton, and sampled a large portion of the pulp stories of the twentieth century. His favorite from the twenty-first century were the enigmatic works of Moss Johnson. He spent several weeks wading through the great mass of western novels from the so-called Nostalgia and Esoteric Periods. And he had just finished the massive tome, *The Fires of the West* by Bojana Michelakakis which was considered the capstone of the Esoteric Period. Nearly one million words in that one. Today he'd choose a genre to explore.

He was about to sip his coffee, but his watch beeped softly. This tiny sound he did not love. It meant he would have to leave his quiet little house, his precious wife, and his reading for a few weeks or maybe more.

However, it also meant he could keep up this lifestyle he loved so much. He swiped his hand over the watch. "This is Agent Omasi." He waited for his assignment.

# 10

"I'M SORRY, MR..."

"Faraday. Mr. Faraday."

"Yes, Mr. Faraday. How can I help you?" The man she saw on the screen puzzled Gwen. Bald but more so. No eyebrows or eyelashes. The two diamond earrings and the suit were probably worth more than her and Liam's condo on Hermes One.

"I heard you were looking for investors for the spaceport on Erebus. Isn't that correct?"

Now she was very puzzled indeed. "How do you know that? Do we know each other?"

"No, I haven't had the pleasure. I just got wind of it as it were."

"And you're looking to invest?"

"Not me personally, though I do find the project quite stimulating. I am a mere representative of a consortium of investors who are very interested in the project."

"I see." More investors would help, but Gwen was wary. "Who are these investors?"

"I'm afraid I'm not at liberty to say. My clients guard their privacy with the utmost security. They can simply be referred to as the 'Consortium' for shorthand, if you will."

Now that tripped something in Gwen's memory. The Consortium? Where had she heard that before? Something with spacecraft or cargo.

"What exactly is the Consortium's business? Can you tell me that at least?"

"Of course. The Consortium provides freighters and other small crafts to hardy and daring souls. It is their firm belief that freelancers are the future of space exploration and commerce. As you can imagine, with this mission in mind investing in your spaceport would be advantageous. It would make an excellent base in the sector and its survival would advance the Consortium's interests considerably."

Gwen sat back. Dealing with masked men was not her style.

"I'm sorry, Mr. Faraday. Without knowing the identities of the investors, I'm not sure I'm willing to make a deal."

"Oh, how unfortunate. The Consortium is willing to contribute a considerable sum. Ten billion?"

Gwen reeled. That kind of cash would come in handy. But dealing with hidden clients? They could be criminals for all she knew.

"No, Mr. Faraday. It is a generous and tempting offer. At this time I'm not comfortable working with anonymous investors."

"Very well. However, the offer still stands. Perhaps something will change your mind in the future. I am hoping to visit the spaceport in the coming weeks. Perhaps you'll have time for a short chat."

"That's fine, Mr. Faraday. But I don't see how it could work."

"Please, please. Don't slam the door per se. Let's talk again."

Gwen was tired, so she simply nodded. "Okay, the door's not shut, but I'm not opening it either."

Mr. Faraday smiled a toothless grin and bowed slightly. The screen went black. Gwen sipped her tea.

# 11

WHY DID WE have to choose these docking bays? Jordana wondered as she threw a shovel full of reek out the bay door. She watched it plummet thousands of meters. The thought was fleeting. The heat was getting to her.

Jordana used the cuff of her glove to push an errant strand of hair out of her eyes. Her work coveralls were unzipped and tied at the waist. Her exposed undershirt soaked with sweat. Probably needed to drink more water.

She knew exactly why these docking bays were chosen. They were located in the eastern arm of Redcliff's great crescent and provided a view of most of the other docking bays. Launches from here would barely impact traffic around the rest of the spaceport. It was just unfortunate that some nesting bird-like creatures had left a three-foot layer of guano in most of the bays and corridors in this section.

She wasn't complaining. It would have been worse if the creatures were still nesting here. By the look of it, they had moved on years ago. Plus she chose to do shoveling duty and choosing to do something always makes it easier.

It was taking longer than expected to move some cleaning equipment from the *Apollo* to the surface, so Commander Cooper ordered the bays to be shoveled for the time being. To get a jump on the setup of the new fighter wing base. Very prudent decision.

However, the order was for only enlisted personnel. Officers weren't required to shovel out the bays. Jordana thought that was wrong and insisted the flight teams help as well. It had an immediate effect on the enlisted personnel. Even now she could see them working hard.

A gang of midshipmen furiously shoveling and scraping came up to the edge near her and pushed a large quantity of guano off. They stopped and looked at her. One spoke up. "Sir, you should probably drink some more water."

Jordana smiled. "You're right, midshipman. I should. Keep up the great work."

# 12

"WE'RE IN GOOD SHAPE for now. We need to get income as soon as possible, but you already know that." Foster finished his report.

"Yes, I'm well aware," Gwen answered. She looked over her team. They sat in a circle on mismatched chairs in her nearly empty office. "How's engineering?"

Edison cleared his throat. "We've made a lot of progress. As you know, we have control of all environmental systems. Crew and staff quarters are being cleaned and more are opening for habitation every day. I'm coordinating with Commander Cooper and the engineers from the *Apollo* on the fighter wing's base. They're handling most of that. My two biggest concerns are evaluating the rest of the base and the installation of the uplifted animal interface. Both of those can be handled, but I need more personnel."

Gwen nodded. "Captain Frost, how much of the spaceport has been explored?"

"Approximately sixty-five percent, ma'am. It's mainly the tunnels, crawlspaces, and service-ways we haven't gotten to yet. The main problem is not enough personnel yet."

"And Dave," Gwen started. "What's your situation with the UAI?"

"The unit is slated to arrive soon. I need more personnel."

"And..." Ridley cut in. "I can't do much until the unit is installed and the flight control computers are up. Plus my flight controllers haven't arrived yet."

"I see a theme developing." Gwen turned to Bao. "Update on personnel?"

"Several transports are arriving within the week. We'll be flooded with people soon."

Gwen nodded. "Good, let's just make sure we are ready for them." Nods all around. Something else tugged at Gwen's mind. "Dr. Pierre, how is Luloni?"

"She's doing well and eating like a Tridarian meta-beast."

Gwen was relieved. "Has any family been located?"

"No, she may be alone."

Gwen's heart ached. The simple thought of one of her girls being alone at fifteen. "I see."

"We may have to remand her to the state." Dr. Pierre was hesitant when she said that.

Gwen thought hard. "Very well, but it's not time for that. She needs to recover. I'll discuss the situation with Ms. Khoroushi." Then she returned her attention to the group. "We have a lot of work to do, thank you all."

# 13

ARI FROST looked over the scene. When Bao said workers would arrive she was right. He stood on one of the large landing pads on the top of the plateau. Ferries, cargo ships, and skim-hoppers landed and took off. People were everywhere.

But it was organized. Bao and he had worked out a plan. As people arrived security officers would scan their ID and direct them to the appropriate department for processing. They'd receive a uniform, meal tickets, lodging, and be informed of their work schedule.

He paced around the rim of the landing pad to avoid an incoming transport. Goods arrived too. Food, medical supplies, computers, spare parts, cleaning equipment, bedding, furniture, more food. Almost everything imaginable.

The transport near him lowered its ramp and more people streamed out. Young, old, male, female, short, tall. Everyone was being civil, which he liked. He stepped up and motioned. "This way, please. Over there at the tables. Please have your ID ready." His voice boomed, the volume increased by his helmet.

# 14

THE GREAT CONCOURSE looked good. Gwen walked through, watching workers polish, repair, and hurry through, heading for tasks elsewhere. Yes, it was coming along nicely and it was reassuring to know that work like this was happening all over the spaceport. Soon, very soon, ships could start arriving, or at least that was the plan.

The sight of Langley Khoroushi approaching reminded Gwen she was running late. "Ms. Khoroushi, I'm so sorry. I got caught up with..."

Langley held up her hands. "I completely understand, Ms. Davis. No apology is needed."

Gwen was supposed to meet her half an hour ago. "Did you learn any more about Luloni's family?"

"Yes and no. I was able to confirm that her parents were, in fact, criminals. They were wanted for a long list of crimes including the theft of a spaceship and murder. But, I haven't been able to locate any family. Her parents were using various aliases. It could take a lot of time to untangle the web they wove."

Gwen nodded. That poor child. "Very well. We'll have to make some serious decisions soon."

"Yes." Langley didn't look happy either, thought Gwen.

"Thank you very much. I'll check in later and we can discuss options."

Langley nodded and walked off. Gwen took a deep breath and looked around the concourse again. So much needed to happen, but it was getting done. However, the wellbeing of a teenage girl consumed a lot of her thoughts.

Her comm chimed. Back to work. "Yes," she spoke into the device.

"Ms. Davis, we had another sighting and again life sign scanners picked up nothing." It was Captain Frost's voice.

"I understand. Keep looking. I think I know who to ask about this."

# 15

TECHNICIANS SWARMED the AI Well. Dangling, swinging, crawling, walking, running. David Mercer walked through the area. All of this was his doing. It was his plan. He had personally overseen every detail of the computer system updates and now the uplifted animal interface.

He stopped near the largest group of workers. They circled a large water tank. The speed at which they worked was dizzying. Oxygen, hydrogen, chlorine, sodium, magnesium, sulfur, calcium, potassium, bromine, and carbon all had to be precise. Temperature and salinity checks were processed by the millisecond.

But the moment was here. Dave knew the preparations were almost complete. "All set, Dr. Gupta?"

"Very nearly, sir," came the response from one of the many technicians. The technician disengaged himself from a group and approached Mercer. "I was just about to call for the unit."

"Proceed." Dave couldn't wait.

"Bring the unit. We're ready," the technician said into a comm.

A few moments passed. More checks. More chatter among the workers. Then the doors on the far side of the ring platform opened. The star of the show arrived.

The star was a large mottled octopus; the uplifted animal unit the spaceport needed to function properly. It was in a tank about six feet in diameter. The tank sat on the back of a six-wheeled omni-directional rover.

Several operators and technicians followed it. The pace was incredibly slow. Can't be too cautious.

The operators maneuvered the rover next to the large tank. The position was adjusted until two large value hatches, one on the small tank and one on the large tank were aligned. With nods from Mercer and Gupta, a connection was made between the tanks.

"Equalize and open the value," called out Gupta. The AI Well hushed as workers nearby and workers dangling from safety harnesses stilled to watch.

Water flowed between the two tanks. The octopus stirred. Then in a burst of speed darted into the large tank.

"Start the interface." Mercer was anxious. Technicians at control panels typed wildly.

It was startling at first. The computer-generated voice took most by surprise. "Receiving signals. Connections complete. Receiving data." Then an agonizing pause. "Septimus online. Awaiting instructions." It echoed throughout the AI Well.

An actual cheer went up from all the workers.

Dave relaxed. "Septimus, can you hear me? I'm Dr. Mercer."

"Yes, Dr. Mercer, I hear you perfectly. The spaceport's computer systems need a lot of attention. What are my tasks?"

"I'll begin assigning tasks right now." Mercer moved to the main control and sat down at a terminal. Now, it was time for the fun stuff.

# 16

THE INFIRMARY WAS a hub of activity. Nurses, doctors, technicians, and patients bustled about. But Gwen was focused on the young girl slurping chocolate milk out of a cup. She looked different than when she had first seen her.

Luloni was clean and her hair was brushed. She had gained a bit of weight which was good, but her eyes showed the most striking change. There was light in them and they were bright, not unlike her girls.

"Luloni, I need to ask you a question," Gwen started cautiously. The bright eyes looked up at her. "Was there anyone else who lived in the spaceport?"

Gwen noted Luloni's reaction – fear. She was afraid of something. "It's okay, honey."

Luloni gulped. "Some people would come and steal things, but they wouldn't stay. I just hid from them."

Partial truth. Gwen had raised four girls. "Okay, but did someone stay behind or live here?"

More hesitation. The girl was thinking furiously and then she blurted out. "Please don't hurt him."

Gwen sat on the edge of the bed. "We're not going to hurt anyone, sweetie. Someone else lives here?" Luloni nodded. "Who are they, Luloni?"

"I don't know. He never talked. I only saw him a few times. He left food for me a couple of times. Please don't hurt him."

"No one will hurt him. I promise. He never talked?"

"No, I only saw him from far away. He never came close."

Gwen was confused but glad this person never hurt her. Luloni looked worried. "Honey, I'll inform the security teams and no one will hurt him."

Luloni nodded and slurped more chocolate milk.

"There's one more thing, sweetheart." The bright eyes looked up again. "The doctor says you are well enough to leave the infirmary."

Fear again. Gwen could taste it. "Where will you send me?" The voice quivered.

"Nowhere. You need to stay here at the spaceport at least for a while." Gwen saw her relax. "We're not set up for someone under eighteen to live alone, so I was going to ask if you'd like to stay with me."

The bright eyes sparkled.

# 17

RIDLEY LOPEZ fumbled in the dark. Flipped a switch. Lights lit up his quarters. Things snowballed after Septimus came online. The flight control systems were being installed around the clock. Getting his staff trained and up to speed was equal to several full-time jobs, if not a dozen.

He had checked on the flight control systems one more time, before he called it a day. Everything checked out. Mercer was good, though a bit... odd. Bao located everything he needed. Soon it would all come together.

Now that he was in quarters, he was empty. On Command and Control, people swarmed everywhere. He had to make decisions every minute. It just wasn't the same without Brecklyn and the kids. They'd be here soon.

He should eat. That made sense, but his mind had been stepped on and thrown against a tree. At least that's what it felt like, and it certainly wasn't working right. Eat. Sleep. Back to work. Don't miss the smell of her hair and the kids' laughter too much. It'd hurt too bad.

Ridley couldn't wait to know how many ships would use the spaceport. According to data Gwen had, there were more than enough ships in the sector to support their efforts. There better be. Oh, right. Food. Sleep.

# 18

"ALL YOUR PROJECTS are proceeding on schedule, sir," said the young man on the screen.

"Thank you, Jonas." Gardner was very pleased with himself. Jonas had everything under control and things were progressing nicely in the corporate headquarters. Noticing movement near his office door he decided the conversation was over. "That'll be all for now." The young man nodded and the screen went black.

Gardner looked up to see three people standing by the wall of glass near the door to his office. They appeared to whisper to each other and then rang the chime on the door. "Come in," Gardner breathed coolly.

The two men and a woman entered quickly and closed the door behind them. Nervousness punctured the air of professionalism they projected. The woman said, "Srinivas had another heart attack."

"Oh no. That's terrible. Is he alright?" Gardner's face reflected deep concern, yet his heart danced with glee.

"Yes," said one of the men. "He's fine. He was taken to hospital near his residence."

Gardner sighed deeply and stood up. "Well, that's good news. Poor old fellow. I hope he recovers quickly." The visitors nodded with agreement.

Gardner walked around his desk. "What's that? Two this year?"

"Yes, sir," the woman answered.

"I feel sorry for him. He's had a heart transplant and regenerative treatments, but I guess it will happen to us all at some age." He paused and looked as though he'd discovered a horror. "Oh, do you think the board will lose confidence in him?"

"They may, sir," said one of the men. "We're at a critical phase and we need a steady hand right now."

"Oh, I would hate for that to happen." Gardner continued the act, watching the faces of the others.

"Of course, sir," said the woman. "But we do need strong leadership."

"Well, I'll contact the board to let them know I'm fully behind Srinivas."

"Absolutely, sir," said one of the men.

"Thank you for letting me know." Gardner moved back to his desk as the three exited his office. He sat down and smiled.

# 19

GWEN WATCHED LULONI stare out of the gigantic window at the falling water. The director's quarters which she had taken over were huge. The large living room window looked out at the backside of the waterfall. The several so-called 'living walls' had to be reseeded, but soon moss and flowers would be growing on them. Those things and several other architectural features created a stunning living space.

What was the name of the architect who designed the spaceport again? Giovanbattista Morello that's who it was. He did an incredible job and had given the director – or now in Gwen's case, the owner – unparalleled quarters. She'd have to look up information about him again.

Gwen moved up beside Luloni. "I thought you could have the second room to the left down the hallway."

Luloni nodded.

Gwen wondered what she was thinking. "It's beautiful, isn't it?" Gwen looked at the falling water.

"Yes." Luloni looked up at Gwen. "I used to come here sometimes and watch it."

Of course, thought Gwen. This little imp had full run of the spaceport. "I'll have to ask you some questions about the spaceport since you know it so well." Yet, she was apprehensive. How would this traumatized girl react once she was told she couldn't do something?

# 20

Goodluck Omasi stood in the doorway. The poorly-lit bar was crowded. Why did people always want to meet in places like this? His vision changed. He added more light; he highlighted anyone who possibly resembled his contact.

He moved into the room, walking slowly. Eyes were on him. He could see that with his normal vision. A flashing indicator light within his enhanced vision told him he was being scanned. He figured as much. That's why his weapon was installed in his arm. It would scan as a bone.

He took stock of the people around him. He was head and shoulders taller than most which wasn't anything unusual. Most of the people wore clothes that pegged them as full-time partiers. He could also see some professionals mixed in here and there, but there were others. Just one or two sprinkled throughout.

The scars near their collarbones gave them away. Long-term vacuum suit use could cause scarring around the left collarbone, if left untreated. Also, their gaits were different. More time on ships than planet-side. They were either freight runners or pirates. In this place, they were probably freight runners, but he couldn't be sure.

Goodluck approached the bar. He caught the eye of a pretty young bartender. She came to him and before she could speak he said, "Clarissa?"

The young woman looked pointedly to a door on the other side of the room. Goodluck nodded and began walking through the crowd to the waiting door.

# 21

"ARE YOU CERTAIN?" Ridley was confused.

"Yes, sir. The ship matches no known configuration nor is it broadcasting standard GU transponder. They are requesting to land."

Why was this ship here now? The spaceport wouldn't be open for traffic for some time. "Wave them off. Refer them to Newcastle. It has minimal facilities."

"They are refusing, sir. They say they need to land here."

Hmm... "Can you put the scan on the main screen?" This was all Ridley needed. The flight operations barely functioned and they were nowhere near ready to receive vessels. Let alone an unknown one.

"Maybe, sir." One of the large windows that overlooked the valley turned into a screen. An image appeared in a green outline. Data surrounded it. Ridley took it in quickly.

The ship was doughnut-shaped. About thirty meters in circumference. Odd design. The power signature was strong. Engines were somewhat familiar, but the configuration was something he had never seen before. Armaments? He couldn't tell.

"Weapons? Do you see any weapons?"

Several nearby flight controllers worked their controls. "No, or if there are, they are like nothing we've ever seen."

Ridley didn't like this at all. "What's the location of the *Apollo*?"

"She moved out of the system three days ago."

Of course she did.

"Sir, we're being hailed. They are offering visual."

"Patch visual through to the screen." Ridley held his breath.

The diagram of the ship disappeared and a man appeared. The gray that touched his hair and beard told Ridley he was about thirty-five to forty. He was dressed in a uniform with the colors of white, gray, and red. The fabric could have been silk or Breslin. No, something else.

Then the voice came. "I am Harrison Singh, formerly Captain in the Galactic Union Defense Force, now an ambassador for the Raceme Aggregate. We wish to establish formal diplomatic and trade relations with the Galactic Union."

Ridley knew when he was in over his head. "Alert Ms. Davis, Ms. Khoroushi, and Commander Cooper."

# 22

GWEN TOOK A DEEP BREATH, they were about to meet a ghost. Commander Cooper, Ari Frost, and Langley Khoroushi stood next to her on the landing pad. The wind tugged Gwen's blouse. The air was warm and pleasant, yet she got a whiff of ship fuel from the adjacent landing pad where a ship was being serviced.

There it was. A silver circle in the azure sky. The fighter escort boomed and roared overhead. She jumped. Her heart quickened as the silver ring vessel settled. No landing gear. It simply rested on its hull. A doorway opened on the side of the ship and out walked a dignified man.

"Welcome to Redcliff Spaceport, Ambassador." Gwen met his gaze as he approached.

The ambassador stopped and offered a bow. "It is a pleasure."

The wind tugged Gwen's blouse. The air was warm and pleasant, yet she got a whiff of a fuel smell from the adjacent landing pad. "We want to welcome you properly. However, we have a few questions first before we enter the spaceport."

"Of course."

"I hope you'll forgive us, but we checked our records. Captain Harrison Singh was listed as missing in action seventy-six years ago. That would make him one hundred and fifteen years old."

"And I don't look a day over forty, so I cannot possibly be as old as I claim to be."

"The thought crossed our minds." Gwen searched his face and body language for clues. Nothing yet. "You look exactly like Captain Singh's service picture. Were you surgically altered or are you a clone?"

"Neither. Seventy-six years ago, during the AI War, I was a squadron leader at the Battle of Leto Prime. I'm sure your records showed that?"

Gwen nodded.

"Excellent, but your records could not have shown what happened next. Due to damage from an enemy attack an engine malfunction blew me out of Galactic Union space where I crash-landed on the homeworld of the Raceme Aggregate. They repaired my substantial injuries and that is why I look the way I do."

Homeworld? Repaired injuries so a man over one hundred looks forty? It was too incredible. The line of reasoning was too shocking for Gwen. "Are you telling us that you discovered..." She rolled the word around in her mind. In more than a millennium of space exploration, humans have never found... "...aliens?"

Singh smiled. "No, not in the sense you mean. The Raceme Aggregate is an offshoot of humanity. They are an entire civilization of nanites."

Gwen recoiled as did the others with her. Nanites? Intelligent machines? An offshoot of the AI that nearly wiped out humanity?

Singh put up his hands in a sign of openness and friendship. "Please do not be afraid. The Raceme Aggregate wants to reach out in friendship and cooperation."

Another staggering thought exploded in Gwen. "You've been invaded by them. That's why you look so young. You're infected."

"No. No, I was not invaded. They asked permission and I gave it to them. I would have died without their help."

"You'll infect us."

"No, no. Please listen. I'm unarmed. My ship is unarmed. Weapons are not needed."

That was directed at Frost and Cooper. Gwen hadn't even noticed their hands reaching for sidearms. Gwen spoke quickly to them. "Gentlemen, stand down." Frost and Cooper relaxed but only slightly. "I'm sorry, Ambassador. AI almost ended humanity as we know it."

"Ms. Davis, you forget. I know that better than you. I fought in the AI War. I watched my homeworld burn because of out-of-control AI."

"Then they have infected you and changed the way you think and they will invade us."

"No. Not true. They have done no such thing to me. I was injured, they asked if I wanted their help, and I permitted them. Entering someone's body without permission is a crime and a capital one among the Raceme Aggregate."

Crime? Death penalty crimes among AI? "I'm – we – are struggling with this news."

"Of course, but I assure you peace and friendship is all that the Raceme Aggregate seeks. You are in no danger of being invaded by nanites. I have no intention of ever participating in the destruction of humankind."

Gwen could see the sincerity in his eyes. Was it all a trick? It didn't seem likely. The AI that nearly destroyed humanity did not rely on deception or subtlety of any kind. They knew brute force only. "It may take some time to build trust."

"Of course, Ms. Davis."

# 23

"THE INTERFACE WENT as well as could be expected. Septimus is adjusting well and handling tasks that would have taken my team months."

As David Mercer finished speaking Gwen marveled at how far they had come. "Excellent work, Dave." But she couldn't dwell; she had to move. She looked across the conference table. "Braeden, anything you need to report?"

"We need revenue, is that surprising?"

Gwen couldn't help but smile. "No, it's not. We've received some more leasing agreements for shops. Still no luck with one of the passenger liner corps?"

"No," Braeden said emphatically. "They all say the sector is too unsafe right now."

Gwen nodded. She'd have to reach out to a few personally, maybe call in a favor from all her days at PG. "Good work, Braeden. Keep it up. If we can get any liner or freight company as a permanent anchor..."

"I know, I have a few more options."

"Good." Gwen looked around at her team. "Is there anything else?"

Dr. Pierre spoke up. "What about our new visitor?"

Gwen knew everyone was curious about the ambassador. "We've extended him every courtesy due to a foreign dignitary. The GU is sending a representative to carry out formal talks. Until then he's our guest and we treat him as such."

There were nods around the room, but Gwen could also see the apprehension. The fear of AI was strong and with good reason. "Everything will work out. Thank you all, let's get back to work."

# 24

THE WATER WAS exactly the temperature he liked. Cold. The pleasant taste of crabs filled the water, letting him know dinner would be soon. He let his body relax and pulled the salty water into his mouth. It had been a long day.

The spaceport was a disaster. Not only was everything old, it was also broken. Nothing like the stadium he controlled on Niobe. That was state of the art. But progress moved forward every day.

There was the first one. He stretched up a tentacle and nudged the crab meat closer. Dr. Mercer was very pleased with his work, yet he did have an odd thought. Why had the stadium sold him? They said they were upgrading, but he could have handled that. True, he was now five years old, but he had been engineered to live a lot longer than that.

The crab was good and fresh. He enjoyed the taste and cleared his minds. He'd need all nine rested and ready for tomorrow.

# 25

THE FIVE-STORY TALL WALL of windows gave a stunning view of the rocky river valley. The massive waterfall created the centerpiece. Gwen motioned, "Of course, this is the main concourse. Now on this side..." Gwen looked away from the windows to the opposite side of the concourse.

The bottom four stories were lined with empty holes where shops and stores could be located. The top floor was a wide observation deck. "Restaurants, shops, and more. At least there will be. We are actively recruiting clients to rent the slots as we speak." Gwen stopped and turned to face the small group of visitors she was giving a tour.

A tall man who appeared to be used to physical work as well as desk work spoke up. "I'll probably get in trouble for admitting it, but I've been in the spaceport before. My friends and I ran through this area right before we got scared and fled. It was a teenager rite of passage or at least it was nearly thirty years ago."

"Really?" said Gwen. "So you grew up on Erebus?"

"Yes, Ms. Davis, I did." He paused. "Do you have an official title yet?"

"I was thinking of 'director,' but please you can call me Gwen, Lieutenant Governor."

"If I'm dropping your title, you can drop mine. I'm Freeman."

Gwen nodded.

An older round man stepped up. "Now, now Freeman, admitting to trespassing can be used against you in the next campaign." He said with a wink.

"I know. They try to use everything against you, Governor." Freeman added.

Gwen didn't know what to make of planetary Governor Mirko Dimitrov yet. He was incredibly outgoing, loved to talk, loved the spotlight, and didn't seem too interested in governing. The cynical side of Gwen said that was typical for all politicians. But that was too harsh. He was old and term-limited. His career was winding down.

Freeman, however, was ramping up. Full of energy. Asking poignant questions about Redcliff. Only a few years younger than her and he was already a planetary lieutenant governor. The governorship would be next. Plus if the spaceport was a success, the GU may remove the Erebus' provisional member status and make it a full member. Two senate seats would be created and ripe for the plucking.

"Gwen, you mentioned the area for shops. I'd like to see if a few of the local merchants would be interested. I'd like to have representation from Erebus involved."

"Very good idea, Freeman," the governor added.

"Absolutely. I want the locals to be invested and to gain the benefits from Redcliff. Whatever you need from me, please ask."

Freeman nodded.

She could already imagine the shop slots filled with businesses and the concourse humming. "How about we explore several of the docking bays?"

"Lead the way," said the old governor.

As they started walking again, Freeman had another question. "Gwen, have you met your neighbor yet?"

Gwen stopped. "Sadly, no."

"That's a shame. Thaddeus is an interesting fellow."

"I see." That phrasing and the tone of his voice intrigued Gwen. "I noticed a number of mining permits issued to Mr. Crow."

"Yes, he's a Tirvanadium prospector."

"I guessed he was after Tirvanadium. I'll have to look him up soon."

# 26

DAWN HAD YET to break over Erebus, yet Thaddeus Crow trudged down the earthen ramp to the shaft elevator. He liked to get an early start because the mine wasn't going to dig itself. Plus being a one-man operation meant if he wasn't digging, no one was.

He swung open the door to the elevator and placed the equipment he was carrying inside. He then went to a control panel on the outside of the elevator's housing and pressed a few buttons. With that quick action, he activated the security systems around his small habitat, the machine shop, and the top of the shaft. Being too careful on a planet like Erebus wasn't a thing.

He reentered the elevator and pulled a lever. With a whirring sound, the elevator descended. In half an hour he'd be at the bottom, then the work could start.

# 27

LULONI BURST INTO their quarters and Gwen looked up from her plate. "Where have you been? Oh, I'm sorry... Running all over the entire spaceport, right?" Luloni sat at the dinner table and shoveled food into her mouth. She glinted her bright eyes at Gwen only for an instance.

Gwen looked at the strange girl. How would she handle this if this was one of her daughters? But she wasn't and Gwen knew she'd have to remember that. Gwen cleared her throat and gave Luloni a motherly eye.

The girl glanced at Gwen. "Thank you for dinner," the words sounded funny around the food. Gwen wasn't happy, though.

"You're welcome." Gwen figured an outburst was coming and readied herself. "We've talked about politeness and helping around the quarters, haven't we?"

"Yes," came the food-choked response.

"I'll expect you to do some cleaning and cook dinner tomorrow night."

"Yeah."

Here we go. "Also, security caught you stealing again."

Luloni's bright eyes went wild and filled with dark fury. She sprang from the table shouting. "No! I didn't! They're lying! By the free lords they—" she slipped into Outer System English and Gwen couldn't understand.

Gwen held her temper back with iron bands. This was a child. A child who has been alone. A child who has been traumatized. "Luloni, there are cameras everywhere in the spaceport. I've seen the recordings."

"No! No, they're wrong! You're not my mother!"

Gwen stood. "Luloni..."

The girl cowered before her. "Don't hit me!" She began to sob. Luloni's waif-like frame trembled with terror and anguish. Oh, this poor child. Gwen felt tears on her cheeks. In the next moment she was next to Luloni with her arms wrapped around her.

"No one is going to hurt you, sweetheart. No one." They both cried. And cried.

When the girl stopped crying, Gwen started again. "Luloni, we can get through this, but I need you to be honest with me."

"You'll send me away."

"No, I won't. But if the stealing continues, the government may insist."

"But how?"

"You need to trust me, okay?"

"Okay."

Gwen held Luloni tightly.

# 28

"ARE YOU SERIOUS?" Edison did not want to believe what he had just heard.

His comm crackled. "Sorry boss, but yes, I am serious. Power is out on level 14 subsection D through level 18 subsection I."

Edison shook his head. That was impossible. Everything should be new in those sections. True, they had extensive damage, but with the amount of work they had done it should be fixed. Oh well, they'd have to figure it out. "Okay, I'll be down in a bit. Before then start scanning every millimeter of that power cable."

"Got it, boss. Wilcox out."

Edison returned his gaze to what was in front of him. He shook his head again. In front of him was a massive tangle of wires that consumed his entire field of vision. It didn't help that he was crammed into a small tunnel that was growing hotter by the minute.

Then he heard a pop that sounded like someone biting off a piece of carrot with only their front teeth. He looked around. He saw a small micro-inductor fuse box smoldering. It spit a thin chimney of greenish-gray smoke. He rubbed his forehead and closed his eyes.

He touched his comm. "Ms. Laine?"

"Yes, Mr. Botani," came the pleasant voice.

"I'm coming out. Have Krakowski and Ahmed take my place up here."

"Understood, sir."

It would take him at least ten minutes to crawl out. Then it would take more than fifteen to go get to Wilcox. He was overwhelmed. He needed to relax. But after all, he was learning a lot and he truly loved the work. Plus they were almost there. So much had been accomplished. Focus. Stay upbeat.

# 29

PIXELATED LIGHTNING ILLUMINATED the mountain top. The thunderclap reverberated with the sound of speaker feedback. The brilliant prismatic flash revealed a log cabin perched on a rocky outcrop. The gable roof sagged under the heavy piles of snow. The wind, like some unseen demon hand, seized the chimney smoke and swirled it to nothingness.

Jonas Crane crouched near the hearth inside the cabin. He let the fire warm him. Constructing this environment took time but it was worth it. "I assume the money has been sufficient?" He looked over his shoulder.

The cloaked figure rocked slowly in a chair nearby. "Yes, I've been able to acquire ships and men."

"Good. I'll need to report some results soon." He looked back at the fire. The flames glitched. Calculating, processing, gathering data.

# 30

"TOO RISKY, TOO RISKY, too risky." Braeden Foster was talking to himself as he paced about his office. No reputable company wanted to sign a docking contract with the great gamble of Redcliff Spaceport. They would wait and see. Wait and see.

Well, Braeden couldn't wait. He needed a win and one fast. The spaceport needed leasing fees. He needed to find either a passenger liner or a freight company willing to lease a set of docking bays for at least a year.

The thought had occurred to him before, but he still held it at bay. No reputable company wanted to sign a leasing agreement, but what about...

Of course, he wouldn't consider it a scam or a fraud company. However, there were a lot of companies that had taken some dings over the years, but still came through. They were legit businesses with a black eye. He walked over to the wall of windows. The waterfall careered wildly into the rocky valley.

He twitched his eye and data began appearing in his vision. "Expand search parameters to include..." he began.

# 31

GWEN WATCHED LULONI place the dishes in the sanitizer. "Are you okay?"

"I guess."

"You're doing a great job."

Luloni took a visible breath. "Thank you." Another dish in the sanitizer.

Learning manners and how to do chores was taxing work, but Luloni was getting there. "Your supervisor says you're a good worker. Do you like the job?"

"I don't know. It's just cleaning stuff." Door locked. Buttons pressed. The slightest hum as the dishes were bombarded with cleaning solution.

Gwen didn't want to push too hard. They had made so much progress. "I understand. Cleaning crews are often looked down upon, but cleaning is one of the most important jobs."

Luloni spun around and folded her arms. "I bet you never had to clean anything."

Gwen laughed. "Well now, little lady, our parents made us clean everything and I mean everything. Besides when I was in college I worked on a midnight cleaning crew. A huge office building. My friends at school thought I was crazy."

"Why'd you do it?"

"I needed the money."

Luloni went to the kitchen counter and wiped it with a rag.

"My parents weren't in the position to help pay for my college." Gwen entered the kitchen and placed several glasses in a cabinet. "But do you know something, Luloni? I learned so much from that job. About being a good employee, about what a good employer looks like, the value of a union. I would not change one thing about it. Was it disgusting sometimes? Yes. When the employees who worked at the company in the office building saw us, did they look down on us? Yes. Yes, they did. But I wouldn't change anything."

Luloni didn't answer. She turned and faced Gwen. "I'm done."

Gwen smiled. "Good job." She looked this girl in the eyes and had a thought. "Have you ever played chess?"

"No."

"Let me show you how. You'll love it."

# 32

AMID THE SHIPYARD, Goodluck Omasi was a speck hopping mud puddles. When was the last time he'd even seen mud? He didn't want the mud on his shoes, but it was a lost cause. He was able to evade some of the mud, but certainly not all as his footfall produced a squelching sound.

But still? What was that nagging feeling? He was having fun. How silly was this? If he told Haryati she would laugh at him. He missed her. He'd call her soon just to see her eyes and hear her voice.

He wound his way through the muddy track and past the towering hulks of spaceships and space debris. He finally saw it up ahead. Hastily, poorly constructed buildings formed a sort of office compound. A sign read: 'Sundara-Fleming Resale'

He must have arrived at the end of a joke because the three men inside were laughing so hard one tumbled out of his chair. "Must have been a good one." Goodluck's voice cut the room and halted the laughter. The men scrambled to regain some composure.

"Turn that down!" one yelled.

The man getting off the floor grabbed a small remote from a cluttered desk. He muted the volume on a screen that blared an advertisement for tinfoil-colored hip waders.

A sweep of Goodluck's vision took in the mess that could only loosely be called an office. Amid the promotional posters for ships and tools, he spotted a movie poster. It was simply the image of a gun with the title *Best*

*Served Cold III* blazoned across it.

The man who yelled spoke again, this time to Goodluck. "May I help you, sir?"

Goodluck kept a straight face. "I want to buy several ships." All the men became noticeably excited. "I saw your ad for the three Dual Wizard Cruisers and a Mark Seven Enhanced Wasp Runner."

The men's faces changed. "Those have all been sold, sir. I'm terribly sorry."

Goodluck already knew the ships had been sold. "Oh," said Goodluck, acting surprised. "That's a shame." Now, he had to get them to tell him who had bought them.

"Perhaps something else? We have a lot of ships," said one of the men.

"We just got a Guardian Balboa with a Liberty Class drive," said the man holding the remote. The others glared at him. He shrugged pathetically.

Goodluck observed every move they made. "Maybe, but I needed the cruisers and the runner. Any chance I could find out who bought them?"

The men shared glances.

Goodluck wondered how long this day's work would be. Well, no use in wasting time. "Huh, *Best Served Cold III*? That was a good movie..."

·

# 33

THADDEUS CROW'S SHIFT in the mine had been thirteen hours, no, fifteen. But what else was he going to do? The mine was all he had. Not only was he tired, but he was also filthy. One of the mining drones, commonly called 'dummies', kicked up a huge cloud of dust several hours ago. Good thing he had on his respirator, but still he was covered head-to-toe in a cloud of fine gray dust.

To top it off, he hadn't eaten in more than six hours. But this was a critical phase in his operation.

He flipped switches on the control panel in front of him. On his right yawned a small tunnel plunged into darkness. To his left was the large finished tunnel complete with lighting and power. He pushed the dummies farther and farther. He'd have to get more lighting and cable down here soon then move the control panel farther down the tunnel to keep it in range of the mining drones.

But again this was a critical phase. After a year of constant digging, he finally got his tunnel underneath the massive lead deposit. Now, the race was on to test his theory.

A couple of the dummies emerged from the dark tunnel loaded with rock debris. He flipped more switches and pressed buttons. He sent these two back up the lighted tunnel. He directed them to dump and then park near the recharging station. He'd do the same once the other four came back.

Two more of the dummies rumbled past him. More switches. More buttons. One more drone came out of the darkness. Good. Only one left and, after hooking them up to recharge, he could shower and eat.

He could hear it coming from the dark passage. The last one. Its wheels rumbled over the rocky tunnel floor. It was just like the others except a green light flashed on one of its panels. Thaddeus halted the drone with a sequence on the control panel.

The green light meant it had discovered something. Probably coal, iron ore, or something unremarkable. If he was lucky it would be silver, gold, platinum, or maybe some gemstones. Those would help defray costs while he searched for the real prize.

He approached the drone and used his hands to sift through some of the waste material. Nothing. Nothing. Wait. There. He pulled out a rock. On one side was a blue patch. He rubbed it with his calloused finger. He felt the consistency. He moved the rock into a brighter light. He spit on it and rubbed it more.

Should he yell eureka?

# 34

WHEN EDISON SAW the tug, his first thought was to scrap it. However, Director Davis asked him to give it a once over before scrapping it, and then there was the tug pilot Storm Pala Maki. She batted her eyelashes at him and he knew he would do anything to impress her. His body language betrayed him when they first met and she knew he found her attractive.

Of course, it was difficult not to find her attractive. Her hair was finely beaten gold, the work of a master, and her eyes were the ice on a mountain stream during the first week of April. Stop it! He had to stop it. It wasn't professional to think about a co-worker like that, besides he liked women with reddish-brown hair and green eyes. That was his profile.

Yet here he was working on the tug well after midnight. Adjusting the engine coils was rough on the hands, but he enjoyed the work. Not the after midnight part, though.

It was a Hosho Evander Nerik Class Model J476596-HX1735 atmospheric to high-orbit tug. Eighty years old and showing every day of wear and disuse. Of course, some scavengers had raided the power core and six of the eight engine coils. Plus ripped out most of the controls, the cables, and heat insulation. Not to mention the hack job that was done on the main vessel tractors.

Gwen wanted to save money and Storm wanted to fly it because she had read about this class of tug during flight school. Great. He'd make it fly then.

The old Redcliff AI had designated the tug the 'Red-Platinum-Ladybug-

Davenport-Damascus-Saffron-00000-33434667669-00124623-57674634-Urochs.' He never understood AI naming conventions. To get rid of those names would have been enough reason to exterminate the self-aware AI even before they tried to burn humanity alive.

Once Storm heard the old designation, she quickly dubbed it the *Ladybug*. For all the trouble it was giving Edison he had wanted to call it *Grendel's Mother*. But whatever, *Ladybug* was fine.

One more adjustment. There. The engine hummed. "Hey, not bad," he said out loud to no one.

"Great work." The voice came from behind him. He turned quickly. It was Ms. Laine. She continued, "Some of the techs have a pool going that you couldn't get the engines running."

Edison was a little sad that it wasn't Storm standing there, but then his pride flared. "Oh, betting against me, huh? Well, sorry to disappoint you all."

"Oh, you didn't disappoint me. I bet you could get it running."

Edison was surprised. "Oh, um... thanks. I hope you won a lot."

Ms. Laine smiled. "A bit. I'm not much of a gambler."

Edison nodded. "Well, it's got a ways to go until she can fly again." He stopped. "What are you doing here? It's so late."

Ms. Laine looked at the ground. "Oh, I was just walking by and saw the bay lights on."

Well, that made sense... Wait... The bay was decks below the crew quarters. Whatever, she may like to walk a lot.

"Are you about done for the night?" Ms. Laine asked before Edison formed a question about her being far away from the crew quarters.

"No, not exactly. I was going to run some new cable before calling it a night."

"Okay, I could help you."

"Oh, well... um..." Edison didn't need help and didn't particularly want help, but there was something about her eyes. "Okay, um... there are a few spools out on the deck."

"I'll bring them up." She bounded off.

Edison watched her go. She was a good tech and a hard worker.

# 35

GWEN LISTENED KEENLY. Edison pointed out the sections on the large holographic schematic of the spaceport. He went through every section and how the repairs were completed or what still needed to be done. Gwen was proud she had hired him.

"That's about it. Oh, I got the tug running." Edison finished. The hologram disappeared and Edison sat down next to the rest of the Senior staff.

"Phenomenal work, Edison." Gwen looked around at her staff. "Braeden, why don't you let everyone know your good news."

"As you wish." He looked around the conference table. "We got our first contract on a lease of eight docking bays."

Smiles all around.

"Fantastic," said David Mercer.

"What company is it?" asked Edison.

"Rapid Lancer Freight Hauling."

"I've never heard of them," said Bao.

"I'm not surprised. They are a small outfit based out of Sabus Prime here in the sector."

"I hope the leasing fee is high," remarked Mercer.

"Well, it's a little higher than their credit rating. We had to lower our standards a bit," answered Braeden.

"Well, don't we all sometimes," Mercer muttered. Odd looks from the room.

Gwen chimed in to break the tension. "Nice work, Braeden. Most everyone is taking a wait-and-see approach. They don't think we are going to succeed, but we'll prove them all wrong. Rapid Lancer got a steal on eight docking bays. They took a risk on us, we took a risk on them."

"Do you have more potential clients?" Ridley spoke up.

"Yes," said Gwen. "Braeden has a list and I have a trick or two up my sleeve."

# 36

METAL OF ALL KINDS, wire, cables, machine parts, furniture, clothing, cedar planks, micro-processors, dishes, panes of triglass... Cedar planks? These acquisition requests were dizzying and Bao had seen enough for the time being. Time to call it a day, watch a new episode of *Star Barbarians*, and sleep.

She was about to sign out when a voice said something in her ear. "Bao?" It was a computerized voice.

"Yes, Septimus."

"I'm sorry to bother you."

"No bother at all. Just caught me."

"I won't keep you long. I was wondering if I could put in an acquisition request."

She thought the question was strange. Septimus made acquisition requests all the time. "Of course, why would you need permission?"

"This request is not for the spaceport. It's personal."

Personal? A UAI making a personal request? You usually had to force them to take a break and tell them when they were tired. "Personal? I don't understand."

"I'm sorry. I didn't mean to confuse you. I'd like to request some clams."

Oh, food. That made more sense. "No problem. I'll make the request."

"Thank you. I haven't had them in a while and I enjoy the taste."

Enjoy? Another word not usually used by an UAI. "Like I said, not a problem. I'll get some for you as soon as I can."

"Thank you, Bao. Have a good night."

"You too, Septimus." She had to smile. Clams were added to the list of every conceivable metal, spare parts, and cedar planks.

# 37

David Mercer threaded his way through the great concourse. He was getting used to the long walk, but he didn't like it. Soon he'd step on the lift that would take him deep into the bowels of the spaceport. The upgrade was coming along fine and the computer system would be outstanding.

The uplifted animal interface was extraordinary. He'd never worked with one this closely before. The things it was able to accomplish were staggering. A dolphin could have certainly done his job on the Proximo. Septimus could have done it with his eyes closed. Not that it needed its eyes.

They were very close to flipping the switch and turning this whole thing on, if Edison could figure out the power outages. Just a bit more work and then it would be time. He dodged a cleaning crewman buffing the floor. He wished those people would be more careful.

Still that uplifted animal interface. There was something about it. A niggling little thought came to the edge of his mind. Did Septimus have a soul? Did all UAIs? Would a war have to be fought with them one day?

He rushed up to the lift and pressed down. He pushed aside those thoughts as he did with other questions. Where did I come from? Was there a God? Did he have a claim on me? What happens when I die?

No time. No time for those questions. He had work to do, so he could go back to his quarters and watch videos.

# 38

"MOM ALWAYS DOES stuff like that," Gwen heard Chloe say and then Luloni laughed. When she thought of introducing Luloni to Chloe she knew they would become friends. She loved Chloe so much for taking time out of her college schedule to talk to this little lost girl thousands of light years away.

Gwen closed the door to the office in her quarters. She sat at the desk. She had just finished going over progress reports from so many departments her eyes were blurry. She clicked over to her news feed.

Standard stuff. Explosions on several planets. A mining rig collapse that trapped thirty-four workers. GU forces prevented a civil war on some planet she never heard of. Then something. She read the headline again: Stock Price Jumps as PanGalacta Welcomes New CEO.

She clicked and quickly scanned the article. There it was. Gardner had claimed his prize finally. He was CEO. What direction would he take the company? What direction would she have taken the company? What did it matter? She was happy here.

She clicked. Wow. The stock price was high. Time to sell some.

# 39

RIDLEY STOOD IN front of Gwen's desk. "Flight control systems are fully operational and they meet GU safety standards."

Gwen smiled. "Good work, Ridley."

He was self-conscious. "I'm sorry it took this long."

"Are you joking? You did a phenomenal job. This place was a wreck and you and your team got it operational. Fantastic work."

"Thank you, ma'am." He had worked harder and longer than he had thought possible and it was good to be ready. "I would also like to thank you for asking me to join the team. I know this is just the beginning but it's been the most rewarding experience of my professional life so far."

"That means a lot, Ridley. I'm glad you decided to join the team."

Ridley nodded and turned. He descended the spiral stairs into Command and Control. Flight controllers checked their terminals and ran simulations. Soon the show would begin.

# 40

IT TOOK HER all day but Gwen visited every section of the spaceport. They had tons of setbacks and issues from day one, but they were on the verge. Everything was coming together. She could feel it.

The docking bays were repaired and being cleaned. The flight control systems were up and running. Her staff was mostly in place. Stores and restaurants were preparing to open.

Gwen slowed and stopped on the observation deck. She looked out over the concourse. Soon ships would be coming and going. Very soon.

She needed them to come. Revenue had to start flowing in or this adventure would be a bust. There was still the nagging thought that the sector couldn't support a spaceport this size. That's what caused Redcliff to fail years ago. But, this was a new time. A lot had changed since the AI War and even the Bug War. If the GUDF could keep the pirates under control... Pretty big 'if,' but she had been impressed with the Defense Force personnel so far.

Yes, this sector was ready to grow and she was ready. She broke her reflection and headed for an elevator.

# 41

AS THE SCREEN turned to black, Thaddeus Crow snapped the thin plexi-pencil in half. The meeting with Metatrex Mining hadn't gone as he planned. They were playing hardball. He'd expected that, but goodness...

He got up from his chair and paced around the room. He stepped on an empty Xi's Slurpin' Good Instant Soup container. It shrieked with the dying sound of plastic. It made him stop and look around the room. Boxes, bags, discarded food containers, packing supplies, nan-tags were just the starters. When had he cleaned last? He couldn't remember.

He had to face it. He was a miner not a businessman and certainly not a salesman. Metatrex was trying to push him around and no wonder. He was a mess. Too long underground. Too long alone. Enough. He grabbed an empty Cromatics box and threw several food containers into it. Time to clean house. Plus it would give him time to think.

Metatrex wanted a sample of his Tirvanadium. They wanted him to arrange the shipment. Pompous jerks, they should have sent a special courier ship. But no, they wanted to make him jump through hoops to show they were the boss. He threw empty Salyc bottles into the box. Well, Thaddeus Crow was the boss now. If they wanted a sample, he'd get them one. Then they would pay or he'd go to Nairaincorp.

He opened a window. The fresh air felt good on his face. He could smell rain somewhere in the distance as the breeze filled his little room. He hated to admit it, but he needed someone he could trust. He didn't have a ship anymore. Most of his was repurposed as mining gear.

Yes, he needed someone he could trust. He opened the door and threw the box full of trash outside. He spun around to attack the mess in the room. Someone who had an interest in him succeeding. Someone who would benefit even if they didn't get a decipence from the Tirvanadium.

With the room he cleared, he could now pull a broom out of the tiny supply closet. He began sweeping. Who could that person be? He maneuvered a pile of dust. Of course.

The Spaceport. A new owner was repairing it, wasn't that what he heard?

# 42

GWEN LOVED THE look on Luloni's face. Luloni's eyes were as big as could be and her mouth hung open. "It's for me?" her voice was barely a whisper.

Gwen smiled. "Yes, it is. The manager of the cleaning crew said you were his best worker and that fulfilled our deal. But this is not a free ride. I'm going to charge you rent and you'll have to clean it up and get it ready."

Luloni walked into an empty shop bay. It was about three and a half meters wide and about fourteen meters deep, including the counter space, a backroom, and a small bathroom. It required cleaning, a deep cleaning.

"I love it," Luloni said.

"It won't be easy," said Gwen.

"I'll work really hard." Luloni paused. "What about stock?"

Good, she had been paying attention during their business lessons. "I'll help you get started with inventory and how to source the material. But! It will be a loan."

Luloni nodded. "I'll pay you back. I swear."

Gwen watched her as she danced through the shop. "I have to go. Figure out what you need and any questions you have and we'll talk tonight."

"I will, I will! Thank you, thank you!" Luloni ran to Gwen and hugged her. Gwen hugged her back and thought about how much she missed her daughters' hugs.

# 43

THE STAFF SAT TOGETHER in the conference room. Dave's and Edison's reports had gone well. Ridley was all set with flight operations. Dr. Pierre had the medical staff under control, plus she had two deputies who were whip-smart. Where did she find them? Bao found supplies and equipment in places and on worlds she didn't know existed. Frost was on top of security.

"It looks like we are all set. A marketing blitz will start soon. We've purchased ads on twelve planets, plus a press release across the entire GU. Not to mention letting all planetary governments in the sector know about the spaceport." Gwen was confident. "Also, Braeden, why don't you let everyone know."

Braeden straightened in his chair. "Well, it's thanks to you, Gwen. But, I can let everyone know. Gwen was able to get the White Peddle Line to lease three docking bays."

"You must have called in some favors, Gwen," said Mercer. "They are a fine passage liner company."

"You're right, I did." Gwen wasn't shy. She had called in a favor. Jet owed her big time and now that he was CEO of White Peddle, it was time for payback. "Oh, we also got a contract in place for a local company to ferry people back and forth to Newcastle and Freetown."

Nods from around the room. "More are in the works," said Braeden. "We'll have some revenue in place for certain."

Gwen approved. "Okay, Let's put the finishing touches on it."

# 44

REROUTING POWER... Docking bay doors open... Regulating temperature on decks fourteen to twenty-four... Access request to Sub Basement 47-B... Septimus handled routine functions. Nothing big yet, but once the spaceport reached capacity, the thing would be hopping.

He stretched and reached one tentacle around a rock. The texture was nice. Something else though. Oh, he was hungry. He made a mental note.

Outside of his enclosure, on a panel, a light turned on. He watched the technician nearby. She noticed, switched it off and pressed a button. "How are we doing today, Septimus?"

"I'm well." The octopus answered.

"Need a little snack?"

"Yes, please."

"Coming right up." More buttons were pressed.

Septimus could taste the crab meat entering the water. He maneuvered his tentacles to grab a piece of meat. "Thank you."

"Your welcome, my good sir." The young woman said with a flourish.

People fascinated him. What would they do next? Just then he noticed another female technician approach, the one who fed him. What were they doing? He listened.

The new arrival whispered. "Did you hear? Some of the senior staff ladies are having a girls' night."

The first technician looked up from the console. "What? Are we invited?"

"Not sure yet. Word just started spreading."

"Ooo, keep me posted."

"Will do."

Girls' night? What was that? What were they talking about? Searching database... Eating crab... Running the spaceport's computers... Having nine brains was helpful. Ah, girls' night... Reading... Reading... Reading...

A familiar face appeared outside the enclosure. "Good morning, Dr. Mercer."

"Good morning, Septimus. Taking a bit of a break I see. Good."

"Yes, I was hungry. Technician Hampton gave me some crab meat. Have you eaten today?"

"I have. Thank you for asking. Is everything else fine?"

"Yes, I'm feeling well and the computer system is running smoothly."

"Good, in just a few moments I'll start today's processing-cycle."

"Very good, but first..."

"Yes?"

"Could I ask you a question?"

"Certainly."

"I have just learned of a thing called girls' night. I see there is a cognate called a guys' night."

"Yes." Mercer drug out the word. Septimus picked up the clue. He was wondering why I'm asking.

"I'm sorry if I'm confusing you. I just found it interesting and was wondering something. Would it be possible for us to have a guys' night?"

"I beg your pardon."

Oh, I've confused him. "I mean, we are males. Some others could be invited. It seems watching sporting events is common behavior." Mercer's face had a strange look. Like a computer processing slowly.

"You want to have a guys' night? With me and others? And watch sports?"

"Yes, if it's not any trouble. Of course, you may not wish to spend time with a UAI. In that case, I completely understand."

"No, no. That's not it. I'm just surprised. I've never heard of a UAI taking an interest in human behavior like this."

"Then would it be possible?"

"Sure. Let me think about it a little and I'll see what I can do."

"Thank you, Dr. Mercer. Shall we begin the processing cycle?"

# 45

Gwen raced up the spiral stairs to her office. The call had been extremely urgent. Of course, she was deep in the bowels of the station at the time the call came.

The lieutenant governor and another man were waiting for her in her office. Captain Frost stood nearby armed to the teeth. The call requested the presence of the head of security.

The man she didn't know was short but powerfully built. He hadn't had a haircut or a beard trim in a while and his hands looked to be permanently etched with dirt.

"Gentlemen, your message was urgent."

The lieutenant governor spoke. "Yes, sorry to barge in on you." He gestured. "Allow me. This is Thaddeus Crow. He's your neighbor."

"Oh, of course, the independent miner off to the east."

"Ma'am," Thaddeus said curtly.

"Mr. Crow has made a discovery," the lieutenant governor said carefully. "We needed to see you right away."

"Discovery?" Gwen tried to understand the urgent meeting and careful language. She glanced at Frost. He was watching the men closely.

"Yes, a discovery. Mr. Crow, could you show Director Davis?"

The old prospector looked nervous. What was he about to say? Wasn't used to people? Gwen thought it was both. He reached his hand into his vest and produced a tiny clear plastic bag with a touch of blue powder in it. "I've worked all my life to find this," he rasped as if his tongue was rusty.

"I'm sorry, what is it?" Gwen assumed he'd mined the substance but she was confused. What was it? Why was this so urgent?

"Tirvanadium, Ms. Davis." Thaddeus had emotion in his voice.

"I see. Tirvanadium is very valuable. I'm happy for you, Mr. Crow."

"It's my life's work. Thank you, ma'am," the miner responded.

"It will be excellent for the local economy, but I'm confused. Why the urgency?" Gwen looked to Freeman.

"Mr. Crow has some security concerns," said the lieutenant governor.

"I'd like your help securing my site. There are a lot of illegal mining outfits in the fringe and I'll need a ship in the near future." The miner was earnest.

"Why come to me? You seem to have government connections."

"I've known Freeman here for years, but there's nothing he can do."

"He's right, Gwen. I'm in no official position to lend aid to a private enterprise, especially one operated by a family friend."

Gwen nodded. Conflict of interest and government stretched thin on a provisional member world. Tirvanadium meant more industry and more space traffic coming to Erebus. "How can we help?"

# PART 3:
# OPEN FOR BUSINESS

Open for business
Set out your all wares to sell
May business be good

- The Poet Loam

# 1

JORDANA SALAMANCA hit the throttle. Her fighter craft screamed out of the launch bay. She left Redcliff Spaceport and its wide arc far behind her as the craft hurtled through the sky toward outer space.

Her scanners picked them up first, of course, but now she could see specks. The enemy ships. The pirates in this sector had certainly grown bold. She checked more scanners; her squadron was with her. It had only been one minute and forty-five seconds since the alert sounded in the spaceport. Not bad, but they could do better.

"Ghost Leader to Ghost Five," she spoke into her headset.

"Ghost Five."

"Take Ghost Six, Seven, and Eight and swing around 687-Point-25-Mark-3."

"Roger, Ghost Leader."

Jordana watched the bleeps on her screen veer off. "Rest of Ghost Squadron set Attack Pattern Alpha Omicron." She watched their signals shift into position.

"Ghost Two, you ready?" She took a deep breath.

"Always, Ghost Leader, always."

Jordana smiled; he was one fine wingman. "Follow my lead."

"On it."

The specks grew larger. Screens flashed. Alarms beeped. Green and blue fire rained down. Jordana flipped switches. "Weapons hot."

"Confirmed, weapons hot," came the reply from Ghost Two.

Jordana pressed a button on her flight stick and red energy death flew from the gun ports on her fighter craft. One enemy vessel was stuck immediately and twisted in ways that seemingly defied physics. She saw Ghost Two's weapons fire and noted he scored a hit as well.

She pointed her craft and punched through the center of the enemy's formation. The blue haze of the sky turned black as she rocketed into space. Her scanners picked up the pirate mothership. She quickly sent sensor data back to the base at the spaceport. They were no match for it alone.

She pulled the stick back and swung upside down in a mighty arc. Glance. Ghost Two was right with her. She then angled and attacked the pirate fighter crafts from behind.

"We have to make them pay before the carrier moves in," she called over the comm and bore down on a target. Another kill.

The indicators on her screen denoted enemy craft were blinking out. Ghost Squadron was cutting through them. Why so easy? She ran a scan on the debris of a fighter craft. No bodies or remains of any kind.

"The ships are being controlled remotely." She quickly scanned the mothership. It was moving away. "The carrier craft is moving away. Base, do you read?"

"Yes." Commander Cooper's voice was clear. "They're testing our strength."

"Should we pursue?" She was eager to catch the main ship.

"No, it may be a trick to lead the fighters away from the spaceport. Stay close and clean any remaining fighters."

"Understood." Jordana fixed her targeting scanners. Only a few more. Time to get anoth—

"Return to base! The spaceport is under attack!" Commander Cooper yelled over the comm.

# 2

GWEN STOOD BREATHLESSLY on the Command and Control observation ring. Alarms shouted menace all around her.

The flight controllers sat helplessly as eight spidery fighter crafts screamed through the valley right toward the spaceport. Blossoms of smoke appeared around their wings.

"They've fired missiles." Ridley's voice was glazed with only the slightest bit of fear. Where are those fighters? Gwen gripped the hand rail.

The impacts shook the tower like a tree in a thunderstorm. The lights and screens flickered throughout Command and Control. Ridley looked to Gwen. "We can't take much more of this."

"I know. What about our defensive systems?" Gwen's voice was hard.

"Minimal effect. These are military-grade fighters."

The spidery fighters loomed closer. Then like a stroke of some mighty sword, the GU fighters slashed into view. Five of the pirate fighters exploded. The other three peeled off with fighters in pursuit. The flight controllers cheered. And Gwen was able to breathe again. "Ridley report."

"Our fighters have them. We're in the clear."

"Thank God. Injuries, damage?"

Ridley touched his earpiece. "I'm just getting some reports." He swallowed. "Several fatalities."

Gwen gripped the railing and closed her eyes. "Where did they come from?"

"It seems they were hiding behind the third moon. The craft employed sensor dampening tech. I'm sorry we didn't pick up the signals sooner."

"It's not your fault, Ridley. You and your people did an excellent job."

# 3

ELEVEN? ELEVEN DEAD. How many more before this was over? Who did these pirates think they were? What were they even going to steal? How were they going to profit?

Gwen stared at the ceiling and then suddenly rolled over in the bed and ran her hand to where Liam should have been. He'd be here soon. She needed to talk to him. Really talk to him. Not over comms and through a screen.

She pounded her fist on the foamkrill mattress. She may fail, but no group of pirates, no one at all, would make her back down or scare her away. Even though it was pitch black outside, she flew out of bed. There was work to be done no matter what time it was.

# 4

"WHAT DO YOU think, Edison?" Gwen asked over the comm.

Edison stared at something out of a nightmare. Twisted metal and burn marks everywhere. The gaping hole at least eight meters in diameter looked out into the valley, but where he stood was ground zero of the warhead detention. Members of the tech crew dangled on cables and picked their way around blackened piles of rubble. "We could probably have them patched in about a week. Fully repaired? A month."

"You have three days to patch them. Gwen out."

Great. Thre days. He'd never even seen a missle strike in person before. But, let's get them patched in three days.

# 5

GWEN DESCENDED THE spiral staircase. She looked over the rows of flight controllers. Ridley paced on the observation ring. Out of the myriad of windows, she could see Erebus' dawn. A thrill made her shiver.

"Ridley, status."

Ridley turned to her and smiled. "We have a line starting to form."

"How many?"

"Twelve so far."

Gwen gripped the railing of the stairs. This was it. This was the moment. "Well, then let's not disappoint them. Give the word, Mr. Lopez."

Ridley nodded and turned back to address the flight control operators. "Redcliff Spaceport is now officially open to receive ship traffic. Controllers, pick up ships and bring them in."

The controllers began pressing buttons and chattering with the captains and crews of awaiting ships. Gwen drew energy from the scene. She moved her eyes over the flight controllers. Picked up bits of conversations and instructions. Day one of a working spaceport. At last.

# 6

THE PASSENGERS DISEMBARKED, crumpled, and bleary-eyed, save one. His suit was fresh and unwrinkled. His eyes were sharp and clear. With a slight motion of his hand, Mr. Faraday whisked a speck of dust off his shoulder.

There. Much better.

His first impression of the spaceport was that it was satisfactory. People bustled about. All good, all good. It was old, but it appeared Ms. Davis had not been idle. However, buildings and structure mattered little. It was the location that made this spaceport important.

Now, he needed to meet with Ms. Davis to see if anything had changed. Perhaps his offer was more attractive now that expenses were piling up.

# 7

GOODLUCK OMASI stepped lightly. Shards of metal debris, rocks, and things that defied classification filled the inside of the tunnel. Cables coiled limply down from the ceiling like dead snakes. In his vision, an indicator told him something was alive a little further around a bend.

When he arrived it was a makeshift camp tucked into an alcove in the dank wall. A small fire hissed, popped, and cracked. Next to it huddled an old woman wrapped in filthy rags. Goodluck approached her and squatted near the fire.

The woman barely acknowledged his presence. He looked at her face. Eyes heavily coated with cataracts. Taut cracked skin. The yellow-tinged scabs around her nostrils revealed that she was a frequent abuser of Shunt.

Goodluck upped his alert status. Sensors focused on her heart rate and breathing. Muscles poised to react in a blink of an eye. Shunt-users could become violent at a moment's notice. He knew she didn't pose much of a threat, but he didn't want to have to hurt her. Play it cool and no one gets hurt.

"They say you know a secret way?" His voice was deep and even though he whispered there was an echo through the tunnel.

Her head turned slowly. "I do." The voice was akin to a crow's. She extended a claw-like hand towards him.

He reached into his coat and pulled out three shiny tokens. He held them so she could see that there were three. Then he placed them into her hand.

She moved her hand close to her chest. Goodluck noticed the trembling. He must have paid her more than she was used to.

"Go down this tunnel for another kilometer and then turn..." Goodluck recorded and logged her directions as she spoke.

# 8

"BEFORE THE AMBASSADOR arrives, I'd like to ask you something, Director Davis." Harrison Singh gazed out the windows of Gwen's office. Gwen studied his back. He looked human, but was he still human? Really, human. She had to admit he seemed as though he was.

"Of course, Mr. Singh." Where were Ms. Khoroushi and that new ambassador from the GU? The liner he was on arrived three hours ago.

Singh turned to face her. "My government is looking for trade and investment opportunities within the Galactic Union, as I mentioned before," Gwen noted a pause. This was a careful man she thought. "We would be interested in investing in Redcliff."

Gwen nodded slowly. "While that sounds interesting, I have investors in place."

"Surely, there have been unseen repairs and improvements that have been needed. Plus the attack? Some more cash in your account would give you more freedom. Besides, we are prepared to make a substantial offer."

*It certainly would help, Mr. AI Demon Man.* The thought was vile and Gwen knew it, but God, nanites? "That is certainly true, Mr. Singh. However, we are good now. Thank you for the generous offer."

"As you wish." Singh motioned and turned back to the window. "An incredible view. Oh, and the offer will remain on the table, as it were, for some time."

Gwen swallowed. Where was that ambassador? "Thank you again. If something changes, I'll let you know."

Singh nodded slightly but kept looking out the windows. Then Gwen heard footsteps on the spiral stairs. Thank God.

Ms. Khoroushi and a figure clad in a white suit that Gwen could only describe as elegant bounded up the stairs. Ms. Khoroushi spoke up. "Director Davis and Ambassador Singh, may I present Ambassador Ilario Ciriaco Serpico."

# 9

THE GREAT CONCOURSE was only sparsely populated. Some people came and went. Others looked at devices or stood in small lines at shops to get dinner. Several ships could be seen leaving or maneuvering in to dock through the huge wall of windows.

Yet Jordana's attention was on the man at her side. He was an enigma to her. He had been a fighter pilot like her. He was now one hundred and fifteen years old, yet looked barely older than her. Nanites? Nanites swarming through him. So strange.

Her thoughts were broken by his eyes. "Let's go up to that shop," he said, pointing to a shop a few levels up on the opposite side of the great window.

"Sure." Jordana wanted to see what this man was thinking.

The little shop was called Fabric & Cloth Emporium and a young girl was folding some pieces of satin. Her eyes brightened when she saw them. "Welcome, come in!" The girl nearly shouted. Jordana couldn't help but smile at this darling creature.

"Thank you. A nice shop you have here," said Harrison Singh as he looked around. The girl beamed.

Jordana wandered in and touched some silk. "I offer great prices on everything." The girl tried to sell. Jordana wondered at the girl. Running a shop at her age? Her parents must be in the back room or something. No, wait. She had seen her picture. Was she that girl?

Harrison moved through the shop touching every fabric at least once.

The girl grew eager. "Is there anything I can help you find?"

"Not particularly," the man said. The girl's hope faded, but he continued. "If the lady likes anything, I'll buy it for her." Both Harrison and the girl looked at Jordana.

She couldn't believe it. This man was just going to buy her something. Oh, please. What would she do with fabric? "Oh, I'm not the seamstress-type. I wouldn't even know what to do with cloth."

"That doesn't matter," said Harrison. "I'd like to buy you something and I'd like to support this young lady's shop. Besides, I could have something made out of the fabric later."

Jordana was confused. What was he trying to do? She thought he must have seen her apprehension because he continued. "Please, Jordana. Let's help this young lady's shop, and I haven't treated someone in a long time."

The girl's puppy dog eyes didn't help. Oh, what would be the big deal with some cloth? "Okay, I'll look around." Jordana thought the girl would squeal. As she browsed she kept a side glance on Harrison and the girl.

"How's business?" asked Harrison.

The girl was a bit dejected. "Not too good. I think fabric wasn't the best product to sell in a spaceport."

"I wouldn't be too sure. People traveling. Many with money in their pockets. Perhaps the problem is not having something unique or precious to offer them."

Jordana fingered some cashmere. What was he driving at?

"I don't understand," said the girl.

"What if you could offer customers cloth they've never seen before?"

"Oh, it would probably sell really well, but I don't have anything like that."

Jordana touched some satin.

"Touch my sleeve." Harrison held out his arm to the girl. Jordana stopped and looked. The girl reached up with trembling fingers and touched his sleeve. Her bright eyes shined.

"It's wonderful!"

Harrison smiled. "It's made from fur from a creature only found on a planet I represent as ambassador. Perhaps we could arrange for you to sell it."

Jordana thought the girl's eyes were going to pop out of her head. "Yes! I mean, we can discuss it. I'll have to talk to Gwen."

Oh, this *was* the girl Jordana realized. Harrison continued. "Of course.

I'll come back later." He switched to Jordana. "Did you find something you like?"

Jordana was still not sure what kind of man she was dealing with. "This is nice." She said running her hand down a piece of crimson silk.

"Very well." He handed Luloni his credstik. "Entire bolt. Have it sent to Ambassador Singh's quarters."

"Yes, sir." Luloni scrambled behind the counter to process the sale. She ran the credstik and handed it back.

Harrison turned to Jordana. "Jordana, would you indulge me again?"

"That depends, I guess."

"I saw an ice cream shop on the way up. I haven't had a Rainbow Toff-Tee Bar in a long time."

Wow, an ice cream date. She hadn't had one of those since Creighton Parker bought her a milkshake in freshman year. "Sure." She wondered what else this man hadn't done in a long time.

# 10

RIDLEY BLINKED. "I'm sorry, thirty-eight docking bays?"

The large man drenched in jewels on the main screen of the flight operations terminal smiled. "Yes, you heard correctly. Thirty-eight. You can accommodate my fleet, can't you?"

"Yes, we can, sir. It's just yours is the largest fleet we've had so far."

"I see, I see. We don't mean to cause any trouble. Besides, if we cause any, I'll pay for it." The man laughed until he coughed. "Hartford, bring me my enzymes!" the bulky fat man screamed to someone off-screen.

Hands reached into the frame holding a golden platter. On it was a little ornate box that the large man snapped up. He flipped the box open and reached in with two fingers. The pudgy fingers came out stained green. The man noisily snuffled and inhaled some of the substance. He seemed calmed and refreshed.

Ridley and several flight controllers stared. Ridley quickly said, "Sir, pardon me for a moment." He muted the channel. He looked at a young flight controller. "You get a readout on the vessels?"

She responded. "Yes, Mr. Lopez. They are all registered to one Joakim Firdaus Vanhanen. It seems he is known as the 'Merchant Prince' throughout the sector."

"Okay, thank you. Let's start working on getting those bays ready."

"Yes, sir."

Ridley looked at his panel and then unmuted the channel. "Am I speaking with Mr. Vanhanen?"

The fat man on the screen answered. "At your service. However, call me Joakim. Please, please."

"Very well, sir. Standby for docking instructions. Each vessel will be contacted by a flight controller. And enjoy your visit with us."

"Splendid, splendid. I'm looking forward to it." The channel closed.

Ridley shook his head. "Let's get those ships docked, people."

# 11

GWEN SAW HIM come down the ramp. Even though there was a crowd of disembarking passengers, she recognized his gait and the way he moved his head. When he got to the end of the ramp, he looked in completely the opposite direction of where she stood. Of course he did.

She hurried after him before he wandered too far away. As she came up behind him, she said, "Looking for someone?"

Liam turned, smiled and said, "No, I found her years ago."

God, she missed him.

# 12

DR. JOHNSTON MOSS sat at his desk reading *Under the Ever-Watching Stars: An Archaeoastronomical Survey of Ancient Cultures in the Americas*. His quarters were dark save for his reading lamp. He rubbed his eyes. He had been reading for quite some time, but there wasn't much else to do since they were running on low power.

A small screen on his desk lit up and a close-up of a dolphin's head appeared. A voice said, "Redcliff Spaceport is requesting to speak with the captain before they will allow us to dock."

Moss shook his head. "What, you're not good enough for them, Odysseus?"

"Apparently not, sir."

"Patch them through." Moss closed his book and pushed it across his desk.

"Aye, sir."

The screen changed. Now, a man stood in a room full of flight controllers. Moss straightened. "I'm Dr. Johnston Moss, captain of the *Acheulean*."

"Good to speak with you, Captain. I'm Ridley Lopez, chief of operations here at Redcliff. May I ask your reason for choosing Redcliff and your business?"

"We just learned of the spaceport's opening and its location will allow us not to have to leave the sector. We need repairs to the main power. As for our business, I'm an archaeologist. We conduct expeditions and explore planets."

"Understood. Information about docking fees and procedures has been sent to your ship. Please standby for docking instructions and enjoy your time with us."

"Thank you, Mr. Lopez." The monitor switched back to the dolphin. "We're all set. Await their instructions and take us in."

"Aye, sir." The dolphin disappeared from the screen.

Moss reached over and flipped a switch. "Attention crew. We'll be docking soon." He flipped the switch back into position and leaned back in his chair. Having a spaceport in the sector was extremely helpful.

# 13

THE LANDING RAMP lowered with a cloud of steam. The *Money Lane* was a sturdy freighter, but she wasn't exactly new. Once the ramp fully extended, Dennis Khan strode down it. He took in his surroundings as if he was apprising each piece of equipment. He was relieved. This new spaceport may just save his neck.

Two others came down after him, a large man with dreadlocks and a nineteen-year-old girl. Khan turned to them. "We all know what we are after here. Let's laser-focus on that first. Then we can have some fun."

The others looked at each other. "Hear that? Laser-focus," said the man to the girl.

"Yeah, like we are the ones who get distracted," she answered.

Dennis shrugged. "Okay, I'll laser-focu." He had to admit he was the one who got them into trouble more often than anyone else.

# 14

WHEN THE NEWS broke, it broke. It hit Gwen like a hammer. She leaned back in her desk chair and watched as more headlines appeared in her news feed. Tirvanadium Discovered on Erebus, New Discovery of Tirvanadium in Nindira Rim, Tirvanadium Sets Erebus to be the Next Aldorus Prime. And they continued.

What was coming next? Gwen couldn't even imagine. She leaned forward and punched a button on her desk, selected a comm number, and pressed more buttons. Thaddeus Crow appeared on one of the desk screens.

"Hello, Director Davis."

"Mr. Crow, it seems your secret is out."

"Yes, it does." His face and mannerisms told Gwen he was angry.

"I take it this wasn't planned."

"No, it was not. Did you tell anyone?"

"Of course, not. My senior staff didn't even know."

She watched him chew his lip. "It must have been someone who works with Freeman. What are we going to do?"

"We'll provide security at your site as agreed."

"What about the sample? They're wanting a lot."

"Give me some more time. I'll find the perfect ship."

"Okay, Director Davis, if you say so. I'll talk to you later." The comm channel turned off and the screen turned into images of Gwen's daughters. Gwen took a deep breath. Ten more things on an already full plate.

# 15

NIGELLUS GARDNER fingered the small porcelain statuette. He had been in a rage since he learned the news. Tirvanadium. Sitting right in Davis' lap. Of all the outrageous luck... A beep. He pressed a button on his desk. "Yes."

"The board has agreed to a meeting time," the voice was calm and steady.

Gardener smiled. "Excellent." He pressed the button again. He set the statuette on his desk. Davis may have lucked into something big, but Nigellus Gardner wasn't done yet.

He got up from his desk and walked along the wall, admiring his plaques. They looked nice against the darwood. Maybe Jonas had some news.

# 16

THE SITE WAS a defensive nightmare. It was completely exposed, not only from the air, but from the land as well. Fortunately the footprint was small. Just a few buildings. Living quarters, machine shop, some storage sheds. The access point to the mine was sunken which was good. The miner had a decent security system already but Ari Frost wasn't taking any chances. He was preparing for war.

He paced along the machine shop's plastigen roof. From this advantage point, he could see all the work. First order of business was to dig a trench and then erect an earthen berm around the entire compound. The machines rumbled and roared. Earth movers rearranged thousands of metric tons of soil.

His other teams were busy setting up the turrets. The DesTron's Talos 47B Mark 23 Air Defense Turrets commonly called 'Hungry Witches' by mercs were phenomenal weapon systems and they had eight of them. These would create a dome of protection over the site. How Bao got them and what she had to pay for them, he didn't ask.

He crossed over to view the access point to the mine shaft. The miner's defenses would remain in place, but Ari had some surprises he'd cook up. He'd have to give detailed instruction to Guerrero, since he was needed back at the spaceport.

He raised his arm. "Frost to Guerrero," he said in the comm.

"Yes, captain."

"Meet me on the roof of the machine shop. I want to discuss some things before I head back to Redcliff."

"On my way."

His eyes searched the trench, the berm, crews assembling the turrets. Let someone try to get into this mine uninvited.

# 17

THE CHEESE AND BACON tasted odd, but the clams were delicious. Mr. Botani insisted that cheese and bacon were integral parts of a guys' night. Hopefully, they wouldn't throw off the environment and his system too much. It'd be silly to die from bacon poisoning.

Septimus looked through his enclosure at the various screens the guys had brought in. One showed a soccer match between Sturgis Hopfeld Club and the Mantus Grove Shooting Stars.

Other monitors broadcast a baseball game, a rugby match, a hockey game, a sand volleyball match, a boxing match, a Sepak Takraw game, a Kabaddi match, a mixed martial arts fight between two impossibly large human males, and something called Jai Alai. Then on one there appeared something different.

"Dr. Mercer, what's that sport?" he asked.

David looked at the screen. "I don't know. Who put that one on? What is it?" He pointed at the screen while shouting to the crowd of men. Several men looked and shrugged.

Then Ridley Lopez spoke up. "I did. It's called Teqball."

"I see," said Septimus. "Like indoor tennis with a soccer ball."

"Something like that," said Ridley. "I wasn't able to watch the finals, so I thought this would be a good chance."

"By all means," said Septimus.

He was learning a lot about human behavior. Dr. Mercer didn't seem to fit in well. He talked mainly with Mr. Botani. That made sense. They worked together quite a bit. Mr. Lopez was able to talk to everyone with equal ease. Mr. Frost seemed to be always checking the doorway in case an enemy assault team was about to break in.

The others Septimus didn't know very well. Some technicians, some computer people, a few security personnel. There was a decent size crowd, but if the gathering could have been held in one of the lounges more people would have come. If the event didn't involve humoring an octopus, he was certain more would have attended.

David and Edison joined Ridley watching Teqball. Their arms were loaded with potato chips, cheese balls, and bacon-wrapped around something one of the young techs called a Kuarura. Ridley simply drank something called a root beer.

"Who's playing?" asked Edison as he handed Ridley one of the bacon-wrapped snacks.

"Brazil and Thailand."

"Wow, two Earth teams," said David.

Septimus listened to them and moved closer to the wall of the enclosure. He thought Mr. Botani noticed his movement. "Septimus, what do you think of Teqball?"

Septimus liked the engineer. "It's quite compelling. The range of human movements is astounding."

"Isn't though," said David as he watched the screen. Edison and Ridley burst out laughing.

Confusion. Why did they laugh? "I'm sorry. What was so funny?" Septimus was eager to know.

Edison looked at him through the tank. "We're sorry, Septimus. Just that Dr. Mercer's tone and his look told us that he was... well..."

"That he was checking out the women players," Ridley threw in.

"Checking out?" That was an odd phrase. He had heard it before at his last job and some of the young female techs here at the spaceport used it several times.

David cleared his throat. "The female players are very attractive. That is all I was intending to say."

Oh, that's it. "I see. Your comment was intended to indicate a suitable candidate for mating?"

"Something like that." David seemed a bit reserved. Ah, mating was a sensitive topic for humans.

"If I were to mate, I would die." Septimus would have to spend some time analyzing the facial expressions of the men as they turned and gaped at him.

•

# 18

"WE'RE SWAMPED, Director Davis. We're receiving dozens of requests for docking clearance." Ridley threw up his hands and addressed the entire room of the senior staff. "Don't get me wrong, it's a good problem to have. But it's still overwhelming this early on."

Gwen nodded. "I understand, Ridley. I know you and flight operations are doing the best you can." She looked at Foster. "Braeden?"

"There's a bidding war over leasing docking bays."

Faces around them showed astonishment. Gwen considered. "Very well. Let's just make sure we have enough for single arrivals."

"Absolutely," said Braeden.

"I know this will be challenging, but as Ridley said, it is a good problem." She looked at each member of her team in turn. "There will be a lot of long days and a lot of hustling, but you all can handle it. I know that for certain. Besides, after the rush slows down you'll all be rewarded." She looked around again. "Anything else?" No one said anything. "Okay, then. There's a lot to do. Let's get to it."

The meeting broke up and Gwen leaned back in her chair. Just two minutes of calm then she'd check her schedule again.

# 19

Nigellus Gardner stood in what appeared to be a white room with giant blinking faces all around him. He spoke. "... and that is why I recommend the contract to the Redcliff Spaceport be rescinded."

A giant blinking face of a man opened its mouth. "If the contract is pulled, what happens then?"

"They will have thirty days to find funding elsewhere. However, the sum needed is so large, I'm confident at worst we'll be able to renegotiate more favorable terms and at best PG will reclaim ownership of the Redcliff Spaceport."

"Why did we sell in the first place?" A giant woman's face said.

Gardner's face didn't betray him for a second. However, on the inside, he wanted to burn the questioner to ash. He'd make a note of that board member. Let's see, Zhen Sang-Hun Gim. She'd be a marked woman from now on. "Moving the defunct asset provided a tax incentive windfall. No one in the galaxy could have foreseen the current circumstances."

The giant heads nodded. Another spoke. "Certainly a renegotiation makes sense." More nods. Gardner couldn't help, but smile a bit. He was winning the day. He had Davis now. There was no way any bank would give her any more money, especially after he told them not to.

# 20

BAO SHIFTED IN her chair. She distractedly poked at a few items on her plate. She was the only one sitting alone. Some girls' night. Why had she even come? It was still early and a few of the people she knew best hadn't arrived yet. She should relax. She took a bite of a long wafer.

The lounge was starting to fill up. Ladies from all the various departments were arriving. Several groups had started playing games. Most were eating or looking around for friends. Bao drank some water. That wafer thing was spicy. Not unpleasant, but spicy.

"Can we join you?"

The voice surprised Bao and she looked up. It was Langley Khoroushi and with her was Jaswinder Patel, the spaceport's chief legal officer. Bao was glad to see them. "Please." She said, finishing a sip of water. Finally some people she knew.

"Enjoying girls' night so far?" Langley asked.

"Um yeah, the food is really good." Bao didn't really know what to say.

"Yeah, it looks great." Jaswinder bit into a chicken wing. Her face showed approval.

Bao thought of things to say. "How does the GU think we are doing here at the spaceport, Langley?"

"They are impressed. I must say, I'm extremely impressed. I didn't think a project like this could ever be pulled off, but I guess that's why people like Director Davis are in charge."

"Ladies please, no business tonight." Jaswinder wiped barbecue sauce from her lips. "Let's talk about something else."

"I'm sorry," Bao said. She was always saying the wrong thing.

"Don't be sorry," Langley spoke up. "All we've been doing is working. What else is there to talk about?"

Jaswinder nodded. "You're right. I've been struggling to read a book and even watch anything. We've been slammed with so much work."

Bao thought of something. "I watched a bit of a show called *Dress or Mess.*"

"Oh, is that the one where the people make their own clothes?" Langley asked.

"Yeah, it is. It would be kind of crazy."

"I don't go in much for those shows." Jaswinder talked around a chicken wing. "I really like science fiction."

Bao tried to recover. "I like science fiction too."

"Never got into it much myself, but I remember liking *Star Barbarians* years ago." Langley eyed one of those wafers Bao was eating suspiciously.

"I love *Star Barbarians*," Jaswinder said.

Bao loved it too. She had only mentioned *Dress or Mess* because she thought the others would.like it. "So do I."

"Really?" Jaswinder looked at Bao. "Who's your favorite character?"

"Captain Chuoru," Bao said quickly.

"Oh, he's so cool. My favorite is Ruta." Jaswinder grabbed another chicken wing.

"She's so amazing. Do you have a favorite?" Bao added and she looked at Langley. The wafer had been too hot for her. Langley gulped water.

Another voice answered. "I like Qig." Jordana sat down at the table along with Storm.

Storm piped in as well, "I don't watch it, but Zort is so cute."

Bao nearly froze. These two? They were gorgeous. Jordana, a beauty with black hair, and Storm with blonde. One a fighter pilot and the other pilot of the tug. Girls like this never talked to her when she was in school.

"I hope we're not interrupting," Storm said as she sat poised on a chair.

"Not at all," Jaswinder said.

Bao didn't know what to say, so she stayed silent. She noticed Langley had finished drinking.

Langley spoke up. "Sorry but to change the subject, Jordana, I've been wanting to talk to you. You've been spending a lot of time with Ambassador

Singh."

Bao looked at Jordana and so did Jaswinder.

"He's wonderful. He's been out of touch with humans so long that there are tons of things he hasn't done in years. He hadn't had ice cream, played a game, or seen a movie in like forever."

Storm raised an eyebrow. "According to what you told me last night those weren't the only things he hadn't done in a while."

Jordana smiled. "I fixed that too."

Jaswinder laughed. Langley's eyes widened. Bao gasped and put her hand over her mouth.

# 21

GOODLUCK OMASI felt strange, perhaps it was because he was hanging upside down. It had taken him hours to get into this position inside what was essentially a great tube of wires. He scanned the different wires one by one. Ah, that one. A harmless-looking green one.

A small blade flicked out from under his right thumbnail. He slit the wire gently, but not all the way through. He then used his left thumb to pull a thin wire out from under his left pinky. He plugged into the wire he cut.

Images, video recordings, and audio recordings filled his mind. He sifted. Sifted. Good. He was finally hitting pay dirt. This stuff was excellent. It may not be admissible in court, but it was actionable intel, no doubt about it.

An indicator beeped in his ear. Time was running out. The breach would be detected by someone. A few more terabytes. A few more. That would have to be enough. He disconnected himself. The indicator quieted. Now, to get himself out of here as fast as he could.

# 22

"THANK YOU, Dr. Mercer."

David looked up from the panel and fixed his eyes on Septimus, that distorted form through the water tank. "You're welcome, but for what?"

"For the guy's night. You overcame a lot of prejudice to have such a gathering with me."

David hadn't thought of it in those exact terms, but it was prejudice. "I guess it was prejudice, but UAIs are somewhat..." He searched for the right word. "Confounding? I'm not sure if that is the right word, but we're not sure what they mean."

"Even though you created us?"

"Yes, perhaps especially so because of that. Although, you seem a bit different if I'm being honest. You are more concerned with friendship and companionship than other UAIs."

"Have you had much experience with UAIs?"

"No, I haven't. However, I've been reading a great deal of the scientific literature on the topic, since working with you."

"What have you learned?"

"Very few, if any, develop what could be classed as full sentience. They usually lack a key component."

"Interesting. Do I lack a component of sentience?"

David thought for a moment. "On the surface, I would say no. I'd have to study your behavior more to be certain."

"Would you be willing to conduct such a study?"

What was happening? He needed to finish the processing cycle. He needed to do a million other things. He needed to get back to his quarters. But, here he was talking to an octopus. An incredibly intelligent octopus, but an octopus. "I don't know, Septimus..."

"Why not?"

"Well..." He didn't have a good reason. He just didn't want to spend the time on it. What else did he have to do that was more pressing? The book in the works could be an excuse. He hadn't worked on it in a while though. Time with his friends? No, he was always racing back to his quarters. For what? Oh god... "You know, maybe a study of you won't be a bad idea. I did notice some gaps in the literature and some studies lacked rigor..." He was thinking.

"A book on the subject would increase your prestige in the field."

That's right, it would. Wait... Did an octopus just appeal to his ego? "Okay, Septimus. I'll see. I need a model and some parameters. No hard decision just yet."

"Thank you, Dr. Mercer. That's all I'll ask"

David thought more. "Why did you want a guys' night?"

"I am lonely down here and wanted some companionship."

Lonely? Companionship? "I see. Who told you were lonely?"

"No one. I feel it. I'm very isolated." The computer-generated voice did not fit with the words it was saying or at least so thought David. Septimus continued. "I find it fascinating that some humans willingly isolate themselves from others. Do you know why?"

David fumbled this one. "No, I don't."

"It seems foolish."

"It does." He was far off now. Wandering in thoughts. Certainly, this octopus deserved study.

# 23

LULONI'S HAND SWEPT down and plucked the bishop off the board. "Ha, got it!" All Gwen could do was shake her head. Luloni had taken to chess quite well.

Gwen had never been much of a player, but this fifteen-year-old girl was schooling her. Of course, she had a lot on her mind and Luloni had just finished listening to a book about chess.

"Okay, you don't have to rub it in." She looked around the board. "Let's see." She moved her rook a few squares. "Get out of that."

"Good move, but..." Luloni moved a knight and smiled.

Gwen drew up her face into a smirk. "Very good, Luloni. Maybe I should read that book." Luloni laughed.

A chime came over Gwen's comm. "Yes," she said reflexively.

It was Braeden Foster's voice. "Gwen, we have a problem. I just got a message from PanGalacta."

A message from PG? What could that be about? "Okay, what is it?"

"They revoked the contract."

The world collapsed around Gwen. Revoked? Revoked the contract? Why? How dare... Rage crashed into her mind like water bursting a dam. Nigellus!

# 24

BRAEDEN FOSTER and Jaswinder Patel worked furiously behind consoles as Gwen burst into the office. Flames and death swirled in her mind. *Why that stuck up, pompous...* "This is impossible. They can't pull the contract."

Jaswinder answered, "It's within their rights."

Within their rights? Within their rights? Words came to Gwen's mind – unkind words. She swallowed them. "What are our rights?"

"That's the question. I've been reviewing the contract." Jaswinder lifted a datapad. "They had the right to terminate. However, we have thirty days to find alternate funding."

"What happens if we can't?"

"Ownership reverts to PG." Jaswinder was calm.

Gwen envied that calmness and tried to channel some. "What happens if we can?"

"A new contract would be drawn up between you and the lender or lenders. The funds would be paid to PG as full sale price and PG would lose their thirty percent stake."

So this is how it was then. "He took a gamble."

Both Jaswinder and Braeden looked up. The question was written on their faces. "I mean, they – PG – took a gamble. Pull the contract and force us to renegotiate now that this worthless spaceport is worth something."

"That would seem so," said Braeden.

"Well, they won't get any satisfaction from us. We're going to get that funding." Gwen set her mind and her voice had the edge of flint.

"Yes, ma'am. I'm on it," Braeden said.

"I'll start as well," said Gwen. "Jaswinder, look over that contract and how they notified us. If they didn't follow everything to the letter I want to know."

"You got it."

Barring some loophole, she had to scrape up fifty billion in thirty days. No pressure.

# 25

GOODLUCK OMASI was prone on a rocky ridge. His eyes searched methodically. As his eyes moved, he recorded video and took still images. The scene before him was quite impressive.

The ancient impact crater was huge and at its bottom was a hive of activity. Several large ships were being prepared for spaceflight. There was a Mark Seven Enhanced Wasp Runner, two wide-based Twilight Wolves, and a Shoshimi Enterprises' Golden Chariot Class Rogue Serpent with hull and engine modifications. Bug War vets commonly called Rogue Serpents with those alterations "Dusters" for some inexplicable reason. He hadn't seen one since right after the war. There was only one reason for those modifications to turn the vessel into a weapons platform.

After scanning, recording, and cataloging the ships, he moved to the people. A ragtag lot to be sure: mismatched outfits, prison tattoos, and scars. Most seemed to be experienced spacers. However, Goodluck did notice some fresh faces. A new generation of recruits no doubt. Kids looking for adventure or ones trying to put food on the table and not able to think beyond a lifestyle like this.

After recording the people he moved on to supplies and equipment. Multiple crates of small arms containing Nighthawk Alpha Series boarding rifles were the first he imaged. Next, he saw crates of Dragonfly III sidearms with Pulse Mantis scopes. Extremely new tech. Certainly a well-funded group. Plus they must be expecting to board or occupy something large with that many small arms.

One last quick sweep. Number of people, number and type of ships, quantity of fuel, weapons all were recorded and noted. Goodluck's eyes fluttered and in his vision words appeared saying 'transmission in progress.'

A soft dinging sound in his ear told Goodluck he had better get moving. Something was heading his way.

# 26

NIGELLUS GARDNER. Nigellus Gardner! For more than twenty years it was always Nigellus Gardner. Clenching her fists felt good but it would have felt better if Nigellus' neck had been between her fingers. She needed to calm down. Murder wasn't an option, but oh that Nigellus...

Her vision cleared a bit and she noticed Liam and Luloni staring at her, terrified. She had stormed into her quarters nearly blind with rage.

"Are you ok?" Liam ventured. Luloni gulped.

Gwen relaxed. "I need more than fifty billion unions in fifteen days. No bank in the galaxy will even consider another loan and, trust me, I contacted them all."

"You'll figure it out. You always do." Liam trod lightly.

Gwen relaxed more. "I'm sorry. I shouldn't act this way." She looked at Luloni. "I'm sorry."

Luloni nodded.

Liam motioned to the table. "Dinner?"

"In a bit. I wouldn't be good company at the moment." Gwen made her way into the office.

She paced and paced. All those banks? They were fools. They jumped whenever PG said the word and certainly Nigellus had put the screws on. He must have. The spaceport was a great investment now with the Tirvanadium. One or more of them would have offered the funding, if not for interference.

What now? No bank but fifty billion. Of course... There was only one solution or three depending on how one looked at it. Faraday, Vanhanen, and the nanites. Anonymous partners, a merchant prince, and – shudder – an AI.

She had no choice. Gardener forced her. Why that... Enough. Desperate times called for desperate measures. To save the spaceport she'd do it. Maybe they won't offer enough to keep it going, but she would ask.

Once the decision was made Gwen truly relaxed. A little dinner and then back to work.

# 27

OF COURSE, Joakim Firdaus Vanhanen would be the last to arrive, thought Gwen. His bulky bejeweled form was quite the contrast to the disciplined Ambassador Singh and the exceedingly proper Mr. Faraday. The merchant prince plopped himself into a chair uninvited while Singh and Faraday refused invitations to sit.

"Thank you for joining us, Mr. Vanhanen." Gwen wanted to get down to business.

"It is my pleasure, of course. And please call me Joakim."

Even starker contrast. Gwen nodded. "As you wish." Gwen wanted to get this over with. "I called you all here because each of you expressed interest in investing in the spaceport."

"Something always changes." Mr. Faraday said the words with a flourish.

Gwen hated being backed into a corner. She hated the idea of anonymous backers, creepy merchants, and nanite horrors. But she hated failure and Nigellus Gardner even more.

"You could say that, Mr. Faraday. I need investors, gentlemen. Shall we talk business?"

"I usually like to discuss business over a meal, but I can make an exception for one so lovely as you," the merchant prince rasped.

Gwen's skin crawled. She still hated Gardner more.

Mr. Faraday spoke up. "Ten billion for a reasonable equity stake and docking fees waived for our vessels."

That wasn't awful. "I'm sure we can agree on a reasonable equity stake. However, I can't waive the docking fees, perhaps a discount?"

"Perhaps." Mr. Faraday stroked his chin.

Vanhanen cut in. "I'm only in a position to offer five billion. The idea of discounted docking fees is intriguing. However, in addition to equity, I'd like a hundred of your store locations reserved for my merchants at special rates."

Gwen imagined cracking Nigellus' spine. Calm... Calm... "A hundred?"

Faraday stepped up. "Ms. Davis, you didn't ask us here because you didn't need funding. None of us are new to business. You need us and desperately I'll wager."

Gwen relaxed. He was right and she knew it. She also knew she could work with them and they wouldn't slit her throat in the end. They needed the spaceport as well. It was the enigma that was the man – if he still was a man – that had wandered over to the window that worried her most.

"Gentlemen, before we move forward." She motioned to Faraday and Vanhanen. "The ambassador has yet to speak. What would your government like?" She steeled herself and crushed down thoughts of hitting Nigellus with a shovel.

The ambassador turned from the window. "How much do you need in total?"

"Ambassador, I really think that—" A swift motion of his hands stopped Gwen.

"Ms. Davis, I know revealing your need would put you at a disadvantage. However, there is no need to worry about that. If you subtract the fifteen billion offered by Misters Faraday and Vanhanen, how much do you need?" His eyes were pleading, if Gwen read them right.

She swallowed. "Thirty-five."

"Thank you." Singh nodded politely. "I'm prepared to offer thirty-five billion plus a line of credit for twenty billion for one percent equity."

Gwen nearly lost her grip on reality. She must have misheard. Even the unflappable Mr. Faraday seemed caught off guard. She refocused. "I'm sorry. That's... What would you want in return?"

"You would be an advocate for my government in negotiations with the Galactic Union."

Gwen's mouth hung open. She had no words. Was she to be the puppet of AI demon lords to save the spaceport? Murder was too good of a fate for Gardner.

"I'm hungry," Vanhanen broke the moment with a bellow. "Come, I can have a banquet arranged in less than half an hour. The best deals are always made with good food and drink."

Gwen coughed out, "I think a meal would be good." Might as well sign away her life in blood on a full stomach.

Both Faraday and Singh nodded. "Excellent!" cried the merchant prince.

# 28

GARDNER SQUEEZED the statuette in his hand. "She did it!" he shouted at the young man on the screen. "She was able to raise more than fifty billion in three weeks without a bank."

The image of Jonas Crane nodded.

"We'll lose our thirty percent stake and a base of operations in the sector." Gardner was still shouting. The young man didn't nod this time. He knew better, thought Gardner. "Something must be done." He flipped a switch with force. The young man's face disappeared.

Gardner circled the darwood panelled office. His plaques and decorations suited the office well, he thought. Something must be done. She'll not get the best of me.

# 29

"ALL IS IN PLACE. Ships and crews are ready. The spaceport will fail. Don't Worry." The cloaked figure shimmered in the light from the fireplace. The small shadow-filled cabin was uninviting.

Jonas Crane's false face gazed at the hooded one. "I'm not worried. You are the one who should be worried, Pirate Queen. Do not fail us."

The figure twitched.

# 30

RIDLEY PEERED OVER the shoulder of a flight control operator. "Are they sure?" he asked.

The flight controller manipulated buttons and switch data flashed across small screens. "I can't confirm, sir. But in addition to the freighter *Gobannus*, an ore hauler called the *Bathala* reported similar signals."

Ridley's stomach turned. "Get a fix on the coordinates from the reports."

"Yes. Sir." Screens flashed, data churned. "Here." The operator pointed to a line of data on a screen.

Ridley swiped his comm. "Lopez to Davis."

A voice answered. "This is Gwen. Go ahead, Ridley."

"Director Davis, I need you in Command and Control. It appears we have a group of ships trying to hide from our sensors."

"I'm coming."

# 31

ONE CRISIS AVERTED, with a heavy price, but just in time because now she had another. These ships had to be pirates. Why were they so set on destroying the spaceport? It was strange. But no time to consider motives. She had to act.

The business with PG had distracted her. She hadn't been able to help Mr. Crow. Now, it wasn't safe to send a sample of Tirvanadium out of the system. They'd both thought they had time.

The smell of the clean sheets helped calm her mind. Liam's soft breathing comforted her. She thought and thought. The room was dark but out the window, she could see a soft glow. Morning soon.

She needed a plan and she needed one now. Get a sample out of the system and defeat the pirates. Should be simple enough. Take it one step at a time. Wait... Was that it? Maybe? It needed more thought. Hmm... Plus she needed help from some people no one would suspect... It'd be nice to get some feedback, but who could she bounce this idea off of? Would he...?

She rolled over and cuddled next to Liam. She whispered, "You awake?" knowing full well he wasn't.

"What? It's still early, isn't it?" Liam's voice was filled with sleep.

"It is but I have to get going soon, I just thought..." She kissed his ear. "But if you want to get more sleep, that's fine."

"No, no. I'm awake."

She smiled as he rolled over and slid his arms around her.

# 32

ANOTHER BAR. These people love bars. Goodluck Omasi didn't like bars. This one was big and classy as opposed to most of the small seedy ones he had to visit on this job. It was called the Phantom Stardust. He shifted through the crowd. Searching. There she was. He could see her from across the crowded dance floor. She sat in a booth with a man whispering in her ear.

She was gorgeous by most standards. Flaming red hair. Eyes painted in a striking fashion of her own design. A changeling dress of Talorian Shimmer Silk. She was indeed the Pirate Queen. All the information he had gathered said she was. Though he had gathered a string of aliases, he still didn't know her real name.

He took a few pictures with his enhanced eyes. He grabbed a few images of the man as well just in case he was more than some gigolo. He'd transmit the data and the job was done. Not that he had any hope the GU would be able to arrest her out here in the Fringe, but he had done his job. Arrests, search warrants, and red tape was up to others to handle.

With his job done, he noticed he was a bit thirsty. Plus this place was famous – infamous more likely – for a particularly flavorful house special.

A seat opened up at the bar and he sat down. To his right was a man engaged in conversation with a woman. On his left was a young hawk-faced man drinking alone. Goodluck signaled a bartender and a house special was brought to him.

The first sip revealed an array of flavors Goodluck was not accustomed to and he sucked in a deep breath. The man next to him said, "First time having a Reckless Thunder?"

"Yes, it is. I wasn't expecting it."

"Nobody expects it the first time."

"I can taste the peppermint, but what's that other taste?"

"Ownership won't confirm, but many think it's Y'yrba."

"Ah, the famed spice from Montoro?"

"You're a connoisseur."

"Not exactly. I just know what I like."

"Very good." The young man nodded and sipped his Reckless Thunder.

"What brings you to Queensland Forge?" Goodluck swirled the liquid in the glass before him.

"Business, and you?"

"Same. I just finished and I'll be leaving within the hour."

"Nice, I'm just getting started."

"Who do you work for?"

"PG, and you?"

"Independent contractor. Special projects that require a certain touch."

"Sounds like we have something in common then. My specialty is special projects, usually computers. Do you enjoy it?"

"Yes, I do. But I don't like the travel."

"That's funny. I love to travel."

Goodluck looked at the man. "That's because you're still young. You missed the war didn't you?"

"The Bug War? Yeah, I was only fifteen when it ended. I wouldn't have had to serve anyway. My parents put me under contract to PG when I was three. I take it you served?"

"Yes, the full three years."

"Were you at the Battle of Barasamin?"

"Uh huh, saw the whole thing firsthand. I was a platoon leader."

"Wow, I always wondered what that must have been like. Of course, I watched the battle. They broadcasted it everywhere."

"I know some guys who sold their cam recordings. Everyone wanted to watch but few wanted to be there."

"Do you blame them?"

"No, not really. I didn't want to be there either. But when your species is facing annihilation, it would be nice if everyone pitched in."

"I hear that." The young man raised his glass. Goodluck took the clue and clinked it. They both drank and stared into their glasses.

"Well, better get moving. It was nice meeting you. My name is Goodluck, by the way." He held out his hand.

"Likewise. I'm Jonas." They shook hands. Goodluck left the bar and moved through the crowd. That Jonas seemed like a nice young man.

# 33

"It's nice to see you, Director Davis." Septimus was curious. It was quite early for her to be down here. Only a few nighttime techs were on duty and Dr. Mercer wouldn't be here for another several hours.

"Thank you, Septimus. It's nice to see you as well." Her face was distorted as he looked at her through the tank. "I wanted to pose a scenario to you and get your feedback."

"You didn't have to come all the way down here."

"I wanted to see you and talk in person."

The director wanted to speak to him? In person? What a lovely phrase to use about him. "I'm intrigued, please continue."

# 34

GWEN AND BELLAMY COOPER looked at the split-screen images of Admiral Peele and Captain Pratt. Gwen's mind was plotting her moves.

"How many?" the admiral said.

"We're not sure. However, we are certain there are at least five ships, but they are sure to be hiding more ships in the sensor blind spot." Gwen was frustrated. Why was it so hard to believe? They had been over it three times now. "I'd like some of Commander Cooper's fighters to scout the area, if possible." The scouting mission was Septimus' idea. It added a nice bit to what she had been thinking about.

"We can start right away," Cooper said.

The admiral nodded. "Proceed."

Captain Pratt spoke up. "Make sure they are not detected."

"Of course, sir." Cooper straightened.

Gwen thought she sensed tension, but dismissed it. "Yes, it should only be a scouting mission. If you'll indulge me, I have a plan." She pressed some buttons on her desk. "I also just received information you should find interesting."

Captain Pratt and Admiral Peele's eyes moved as if they were reading something off-screen.

"Outstanding," the admiral breathed.

A wide smile grew on Captain Pratt's face. "Where did you get this intel?"

"A girl has a right to some secrets." Gwen fixed her gaze on them, "Now, gentlemen. Here's my plan."

# 35

CAPTAIN FROST nearly leapt up the stairs. He's a good man, Gwen thought. He approached her desk with military precision. "You sent for me?"

"Yes, Captain Frost. Please sit down. I need you to oversee the security at the mine personally. I have reason to believe the location of the mine was compromised."

Frost nodded. "Understood."

Gwen looked him in the eye. "I have a plan to deal with the pirates. Let me explain." Captain Frost listened intently.

# 36

DENNIS KHAN, Johnston Moss, and Thaddeus Crow all sat in Gwen's office. Gwen's head was down, looking at something on her desk. She was gathering thoughts and crafting rogue ideas into something bigger. She had to make sure she called in the right people.

This was a test. A test of her leadership. A test to whether or not the spaceport would be a success or a failure. She had to get it right. The occasion called for bold action. Now was the time.

She looked up. "Sorry for the awkward pause, gentlemen. I know this is a critical moment for Mr. Crow."

"I need to get a sample out of the system, but with the pirates..." Mr. Crow looked worried.

"I know. That's why I called you three here."

"You think we can help? Frankly, ma'am, with not being able to leave the system, I'm having a hard time putting food on the table," said Khan.

"I'm willing to help, but I don't know how I can do anything," said Moss.

"Don't worry, I have a plan and you'll be well compensated. Besides, Mr. Faraday said you two would be more than willing to help."

Khan and Moss looked at each other. "If that's the case, what do you need?" Khan bite his lip.

"Just give the word," Moss chimed in.

What did Faraday have on these two? Oh, their ships of course. "Thank you, here's the plan."

# 37

"YOU HAVE NO RIGHT to confine our ships here!" yelled Dennis Khan. His face took up most of the main screen in Command and Control. The flight controllers were all staring at the screen.

Ridley rubbed his hand over his face. "Sir, I told you. Director Davis and the Spaceport Authority have issued a ban on departures while critical repairs are made."

"Unacceptable! I'm a registered free trader. I can come and go as I please."

"Captain Khan, this is an emergency—"

A flight controller interrupted, "He's left the docking bay."

Ridley couldn't believe this. "Captain, return to the docking bay immediately." Out of the corner of his eye, he noticed Gwen come down the stairs. She stood beside him.

"What's wrong?" she asked.

"Captain Khan feels rules do not apply to him. He's trying to leave even though you issued a ban on departures."

"I see," said Gwen. She looked at the screen. "Captain Khan, if you defy spaceport protocols it could lead to a lifetime ban."

Ridley thought Khan would come around with that threat, but no such luck. "I'm a free trader. I've had enough of you and your spaceport."

Out the ring of windows, Ridley saw the *Money Lane* rise and prepare to leave the atmosphere. "You're putting your ship and your life at risk. We need to make repairs before anyone can leave."

"Say whatever you like, but I'm not anyone's servant. I come and go when I please."

What was this guy thinking? Of course, the repairs were just a story Gwen had told him to tell everyone. They didn't need to know about the pirates yet. However, this jerk was going to fly right into them. Why couldn't he follow the rules?

Another flight controller spoke up, "Director Davis, you have an urgent communication from one Thaddeus Crow."

"Split screen," Gwen said. The image of Khan shrank and shared the screen with Thaddeus Crow. What was happening now? thought Ridley.

As soon as Crow's image was on the screen he began yelling. "That crooked no good lair!"

"Mr. Crow, please," begged Gwen. "What is it?"

"Some lying freighter captain called Khan stole three tons of Tirvanadium from me!"

Ridley understood now. That was it. That sleazy Khan was a thief and he was trying to get away. Ridley looked at Gwen. She looked shocked. "That's worth a fortune. We'll catch him." She turned to Ridley. "Have the fighter wing bring Mr. Khan back."

"With pleasure." He turned to a panel. "Operations to fighter wing control. Please intercept the *Money Lane* and escort her back to the station."

A voice answered. "Understood, launching fighters."

On the screen, Khan was visibly shaken. "You wouldn't dare. I've done no such thing. That old man is the liar!"

Crow yelled back. "You're a thief! Now, bring back my property!"

"Not on your life," said Khan as his image disappeared.

"He's making a break for it," said a flight control operator. "He'll be in open space in less than twenty seconds."

"Where are those fighters?" Ridley checked his panel. They hadn't launched yet? That's impossible. Oh, wait there they go. What took them so long?

"Director Davis, you have to do something," Crow continued to shout.

"We're doing everything we can, Mr. Crow." Gwen was calm, but Ridley was getting upset. He knew he needed to stay calm, but this was outrageous.

Ridley checked his panel. "The fighters weren't able to catch the *Money Lane* before it broke orbit." He didn't understand it. They should have had him. Wait... There was something else. "Cut comms," he commanded. The image of Crow disappeared. "Director Davis, the..."

Things happened very quickly. On his scope he saw several things happen at once. A group of the pirate vessels left their hiding place and set a course for the *Money Lane*. The fighters broke off the *Money Lane* and headed straight for the pirate vessels. A large ship – the *Apollo* – with several other ships dropped to sub-light near where the rest of the pirate fleet was hiding. A battle. "Director Davis..." Ridley started again but trailed off.

Then a flight control operator called out, "The *Acheulean* is requesting permission to leave on a secured channel."

Ridley snapped his head up from the panel. "Denied." Something stopped him. Gwen's hand was on his arm.

"I'm sorry, Ridley." She looked up. "Permission for the *Acheulean* to leave dock is granted."

The flight operator was confused but signaled to the *Acheulean*. Ridley looked at Gwen. "What is going on?"

"It's okay, Ridley. Everything went according to my plan. I'm sorry I couldn't tell you. Let's watch the show." She looked down at a flight controller. "Put the system scan on the main screen."

The main screen changed to a map layout with indicators for various ships and vessels. The scene was chaotic. Lights blipped and flashed. Ridley knew what was happening. The pirates were being destroyed. He watched one indicator disappear off the read-out. "The *Acheulean* slipped out of the system," he said.

"Good," said Gwen. "All according to—"

"—plan," Ridley finished.

Gwen smiled at him. "Mr. Crow and his sample of Tirvanadium are onboard."

"And Captain Khan?"

"A great acting job, don't you think?"

"Yes, it was."

"Security learned the pirates were monitoring our flight control communications."

Oh... Ridley nodded slowly. "You set all this up?"

"Yes, but I had a lot of help. Look." She turned her attention to the screen.

Ridley looked. The pirates were either destroyed or trying to flee. Fleeing ships weren't getting far. They would be destroyed.

"Transmission from the *Apollo*," a flight controller yelled.

"On screen," Ridley beat Gwen to it.

The screen changed and Captain Pratt appeared. "Director Davis, pirate forces are crushed. We've already started cleanup operations."

"Excellent, Captain. Thank you."

"Thank you," said Pratt. "The information you provided helped us immensely. In addition to destroying the fleet here, we were able to take out several bases as well."

"Glad to help. We would have been out of business if it hadn't been for you."

"Then we both helped each other. Did the sample of Tirvanadium get out of the system?"

"Yes, it did."

"Outstanding. I still have some work to do."

"Of course, Captain.

Pratt nodded and his face disappeared. Gwen looked to Ridley. "Catch all of that?"

His head was spinning a bit. "Yes, ma'am." He wanted to sit down. But then there was something. He touched his earpiece. "The mine was attacked. They are requesting back up."

"Get the *Apollo* back and contact the fighter wing. See what they can do."

"Yes, ma'am."

# 38

JORDANA SALAMANCA nudged the stick to correct her heading slightly. There. She spotted it on her scopes then she saw the smoke. The mining compound was just ahead. She could see debris from what appeared to be airborne craft.

"Ghost Leader to Base. There's been a battle, but it appears to be over. Slowing to take a closer look."

"Roger, stay sharp."

She maneuvered her fighter to observe the compound and switched over to vertical mode. Definitely had been a battle. Several armored vehicles lay on their sides at the crest of an earthen berm. They belched black smoke into the clear Erebus sky. A fighter craft had gone down and sheared off part of one of the buildings. The wreckage now burned intensely in a heap.

She saw people as well. She could tell the Redcliff security officers had prevailed, but something was strange. There was a group of them in a circle around something.

"Ghost Leader to Base. Send medical evac now."

"Understood."

# 39

GWEN AND HER TEAM were gathered in the conference room. There was an empty seat.

"Arrangements have been made to send Captain Frost's body to his sister." Gwen looked around at the faces of her team. "By all reports, Captain Frost's actions prevented the pirates from gaining access to the mine and saved the lives of several of his officers in the process. He died a hero," Gwen paused.

"Can we do anything for his sister?" Braeden Foster spoke up.

"I can pass along her contact information to anyone who wants it," said Gwen. Braeden simply nodded as did the others. "Well, that's enough for today. You've all done an amazing job. Thank you."

As the meeting broke up, Gwen was slow to leave. She needed to think.

# 40

GOODLUCK SIPPED the hot coffee enjoying every part of the experience. The heat, the aroma, the bittersweet taste, the breakfast nook, the sun on his back through the windows.

His watch rumbled on his wrist. Gently he sat the coffee cup down and peered at the tiny screen. A notification from his bank. Five hundred thousand unions had been deposited into his account.

Before he could reach for his coffee, the watch rumbled again. This time it was a message. It read: 'Payment sent. Thanks for the hard work, Gwen.'

He picked up his coffee and took another sip. He savored the taste. Then he heard them. The soft footfalls approached. There it was. The gentle kiss on his cheek. He watched his wife as she left the bungalow.

Another sip of coffee. What would he read today?

# 41

THE PORCELAIN STATUETTE slivered into a shower of tiny sparkles as it collided with the darwood wall. Nigellus Gardner spun around, locking his fierce gaze on the screen. The young man on the screen wavered only for an instance and then was calm again.

Gardner roared. "They censured me! The board censured me! It cost me a bonus of half a billion unions!" The young man on the screen stayed silent. He simply stared. Gardener liked that about him. Jonas knew when not to speak.

"I may have lost the most strategic spaceport in an up and coming sector, but I'm nowhere near finished," Gardner continued, whipping about. His mind turned over ideas, plots, strategies, tactics, everything he had in his toolkit. "We need to get PG back into the sector."

The young man on the screen nodded. "Yes, sir."

Gardner flipped off-screen. No, he wasn't done. Not anywhere near it.

# 42

GWEN LET THE steam and warmth of the shower envelop her. She breathed in and out. She was able to cry and no one could see her. A thousand years of care spilled from her with each breath and every tear.

She couldn't ask for a better staff. The crucible of the last year made them all family. And yet, how could she put the deaths behind her? Frost and more? She'd have to somehow, if she was going to lead the spaceport.

There would be more than enough challenges ahead, but she could handle them. Strike that. The team and she together could handle it. Now, she had to pull herself together.

# 43

THE SPACEPORT BUSTLED. The hallways were clean and fresh. The rows of shops buzzed with customers. Out of the giant windows the sight of ships arriving and departing was awe-inspiring.

Gwen walked briskly with purpose through her domain. She liked the activity. She fed on it. All the new businesses. All the trade. She smiled and slowed her pace. She was on the observation deck above the main concourse and all the spaceport was before her.

She stopped and leaned on the railing. Could it truly be? All this. All of this a result of her decision to buy the spaceport? It was staggering to imagine what a person could accomplish with a good team and a loving family behind them.

A presence came close to her. She looked over to see a figure leaning on the railing only a foot from her.

The man, if it was a man, was shrouded in the old traveling robes of a monk or some other clerical order. Trace evidence proved the robes had been green but now they appeared black. The hems were worn and showed the marks of many hand-stitched repairs. Yet, the robes weren't dirty at all. They were just old, perhaps ancient. The gloves the figure wore were well creased and looked as if they were not often removed.

Gwen wasn't afraid, even though others may have been. She knew at least a hundred cameras had them in view at this very moment. Besides, she could handle herself.

Who was this person? A Far Traveler? There were stories of those who lost themselves in the vastness of space, always searching for something.

"What do you think? Not the rival of the spaceports along the Innerband or Attis Dome or New Congo, but it has a charm about it. Wouldn't you agree?" Gwen thought this may trigger a conversation.

The figure's head rotated slowly toward her. She could now see the face. The face, the face, the face. Not ancient like the robes. It was the face of a young man, but impossibly young or unnaturally young.

The face was friendly and inviting, yet the eyes. Oh, the eyes. Blue rings of fire circled the pupils. The eyes held time within them and a depth of sadness that made Gwen catch her breath.

The voice, melodious and strong, made Gwen blink.

"From ruins, new life.

Once desolate is reborn.

With rebirth comes pain."

Gwen was speechless. The face smiled at her and then moved away. She watched the man until he disappeared around a corner.

# 44

GWEN STEPPED OFF the elevator and onto the ring above Command and Control. Ridley was busy overseeing controllers. He looked up and gave her a nod. All the controllers were busy guiding ships in and out.

"Status, Ridley?" she inquired.

"Systems functioning properly." He smiled. "Lots of traffic today."

"Keep up the good work." Gwen was pleased. Ridley nodded and checked some screens then continued walking among the rows of controllers. Gwen stepped up on the stairs leading to her office. She took in the view again then hopped up the stairs.

She followed her morning routine by checking the news first. The headlines struck her. Erebus Tirvanadium Purest Ever. Nindira Rim Sector Poised to Boom with Tirvanadium Discovery. New Tirvanadium Will Increase FTL Travel by 13%. So-Called Pirate Queen Found Dead on Norwich. GU Forces Break Pirates in Nindira Rim. And they went on.

Purest ever? Increase FLT? It seemed like the news hit her harder than the surprise election of President Webb or even the Bug War. It probably just felt like that because she was at the center of this news story. This wasn't just good for the local economy, this sector was going to boom. And the center was Redcliff Spaceport.

Still processing, she checked her messages. Only eight hundred and nineteen new ones since yesterday. Dave had started running a sentience study on Septimus. What? He should have asked permission. Another one caught her eye. It was from Ambassador Singh. She would have to make good on her promise to him soon. Help convince the GU to accept relations with AI? How had she been forced into this?

Her comm chime cut the thought off. "Yes?"

"Gwen, it's Edison. I'm sorry, but we have another power outage. Nearly all of C Deck. I have teams on it."

"Okay, keep me posted."

"Again sorry, we'll do our best."

"I know you will. Gwen out." Starting the day off with a bang, huh?

Another comm chime. "Yes?"

"Director Davis, this is Langley. I was able to find one of Luloni's family members, an uncle... But, he has an extensive criminal record."

Gwen took a deep breath. "I see." She rolled thoughts over and over. She loved this girl. "I'll come and see you later, if that's okay."

"Of course. Anytime."

"Thank you, Gwen out." When it rains it pours.

Quickly before another interruption, she made a few notes.

Agent Omasi's work was excellent but he couldn't determine who was funding the pirates. She needed to find that source of cash or the spaceport may never be free of them. They never located the individual who had lived in the spaceport despite searching it top to bottom. Who was he?

She needed a plan to develop the three hundred square miles around the spaceport, some of which may contain Tirvanadium. Either the lieutenant governor or someone on his staff had leaked the news about the Crow's discovery and may have tipped off the pirates as well. That needed attention.

The fighter wing was indispensable, but the spaceport needed military-grade defensive systems. She had to get them fast and quietly. She'd have to talk with Bao and the chief of secur—

She stopped and looked out the windows. She let out a heavy sigh. Another note: Write a personal letter to Ari's sister before the end of the day.

## THE END

# READ MORE

Read more about Gwen, the Redcliff Spaceport, and learn when new books in the series are published at www.scoundrelspace.com.

# ABOUT THE AUHTOR

M. Scott Davids is a writer, creator of tabletop role-playing game resource books, podcast host, and a former filmmaker. He lives in Missouri with his wife and their four children. His bookshelves groan under the weight of classic literature, science fiction, and fantasy. He enjoys playing *Dungeons & Dragons*, studying cinema and philosophy, and knows more about 80s post-apocalyptic movies than any reasonable person should. Learn more at mattdavids.com.

Made in the USA
Columbia, SC
29 July 2022